"Why don't call the pol...

Leslie couldn't understand how a man who looked so strong and honest could be so determined to mistrust her.

"For several reasons," Duke answered. "I want to teach Cliveden Phillips that I'm not someone to try this kind of nonsense on. And I don't want to see you in any trouble. I think this is probably your first real mistake. I doubt you're headed for a life of crime. So I'll just keep you with me until you give me the information I want.

"But there isn't any to give! Why won't you believe me?"

"Mainly because Phillips's man is still out there." He turned Leslie's face toward his. "If you can explain why he's following me, then unless it's to find me in a very compromising position, I'll be glad to let you go." He smiled roguishly. "Well, maybe not glad . . ."

Katherine Arthur is full of life. She describes herself as a writer, research associate (she works with her husband, a research professor in experimental psychology), farmer, housewife, proud mother of five and a grandmother to boot. The family is definitely full of overachievers. But what she finds most interesting is the diversity of occupations the children have chosen—sports medicine, computers, finance and neuroscience (pioneering brain tissue transplants), to name a few. Why, the possibilities for story ideas are practically limitless.

Books by Katherine Arthur

HARLEQUIN ROMANCE
2755—CINDERELLA WIFE

Road to Love

Katherine Arthur

Harlequin Books

TORONTO • NEW YORK • LONDON
AMSTERDAM • PARIS • SYDNEY • HAMBURG
STOCKHOLM • ATHENS • TOKYO • MILAN

ISBN 0-373-02821-0

Harlequin Romance first edition March 1987

CHAPTER ONE

"I LOVE IT, LESLIE. You made the old Eagle look like he can really fly. It's by far the best press-release photo I've ever had." The flamboyant lawyer's voice came through the telephone with its famous booming resonance.

"Thank you, Loren. That's high praise from a ground bird," Leslie Lyon replied with a chuckle. "Or is Eagle-1 about to sprout wings?"

"Now don't *you* start in on me, my dear," Loren Barstow scolded good-naturedly. His refusal to have anything to do with aircraft was the butt of many jokes by talk-show hosts from coast to coast, as was his immense stretch limousine, bearing the special license plate Eagle-1, in which he flew to keep up his peripatetic speaking schedule. "You know what I always say: 'If God had intended man to fly...'"

"He would have given him wings," Leslie finished for him. "I still don't see how you keep up your schedule without flying."

"Organization, my dear, organization. Now how much do I owe you for making me look far better than God ever intended?"

Hmm. Leslie thought quickly. If Loren was really that pleased and he spread the word of her skill, she'd be more than repaid.

"Not a penny," she replied. "What are old friends for?"

Loren Barstow chuckled. "Smart girl. I'll see that everyone knows it was you who performed the miracle."

While Leslie almost choked at having been so transparent to the clever old lawyer, he went on, "Have you had any word on your photograph book of children yet?"

"*Children of the World?* No, but I'm getting closer. I have an appointment to have lunch today with a publisher at his estate on Long Island. I think it's almost set."

"Wonderful! I'd wish you good luck, but I don't think you need it. Your way with faces is truly remarkable. Well, I won't keep you longer. I'm on a tight schedule. I'm about to leave for a speaking tour of six cities in five days between Columbus and St. Louis, then on south to Memphis—" he paused for a breath "—and I expect you think you've got to spend an extra hour or two making yourself look gorgeous for your appointment, although, if your publisher friend has the same weakness for red hair and green eyes that I do, it's wasted time. Give my love to your parents next time you talk to them."

"I will," Leslie promised. "Bye, Loren."

She hung up the phone, feeling a definite boost in morale from her chat with the eminent barrister. She was anxious about making a good impression on the publisher, although basically she knew it was her photographs of children from many countries of the world that would speak for her. She glanced at her wall clock.

"Nine already," she muttered. "I'd better get a move on." First of all she needed to get a rental car. She had sold her own when she moved to New York City, finding the expense of storing a car uneconomical when she was out of town so often. She flipped through the classified directory to the pages of rental agencies and then paused, frowning. She would make a lot better impression if she drove something besides her usual rent-a-wreck vehicle, but a fancy car would cost a lot. However, there was one other possibility—Ted and Melody's shiny red Corvette! Why not? Leslie reached for the telephone and punched out her sister's number. With the new baby, Melody wouldn't be using the car, and her husband, an actor in a daytime soap opera, was at work.

"Hi, Melody, how's Jeffie?" she greeted her younger sister moments later. She was answered by a stream of descriptions of everything from the baby's colic to the number of diapers he needed, and was unable to even get a word in about her mission.

Sometimes, Leslie thought with a sigh as Melody went on and on, *I don't think that girl was cut out for motherhood.* Melody had always been scatterbrained. Now she was going to have to either get organized or die trying. Finally Leslie had to break in.

"Listen, hon, I need to ask you something." She made her request, which was quickly granted, and then listened for another ten minutes before she could get away.

Now I've really got to fly, Leslie thought as she scurried to her bedroom and picked out a suitable outfit for an early March day, a deep green wool suit and gold sweater. Then she dashed in to shower and put on a bit of makeup to accent those eyes that Loren had mentioned, vigorously brushing the red-gold curls that flew in abandon about her heart-shaped face, no matter what she tried to do with them. By ten-thirty she was at Melody's apartment. By ten forty-five she was driving out of the underground parking garage. According to the car radio it was precisely 11:00 a.m. when the traffic light turned green and she pulled away from the corner and saw the car coming toward her from her left. It was only milliseconds later when she knew there was no room to dodge—she was going to be hit.

"REALLY, I'M FINE!" she said that evening as Melody and Ted hovered anxiously by her hospital bed. "It's just a cut on my arm and a little bump on the head. They're only holding me overnight to be extra careful." Poor Ted looked as if he should be the one in the hospital. He had learned that afternoon that his soap opera was being dropped by the network.

"It's just terrible. That *awful* man," Melody said dramatically. "They shouldn't allow people like that to drive."

"Especially when they don't have insurance," Ted said. "But don't worry, ours covers everything."

"That's good," Leslie said with a smile. Then she noticed that Melody's face had suddenly gone as pale as a ghost. "What's wrong, Melody?"

"The insurance! Oh, my God. I don't think—" Melody rummaged in her purse and drew out her checkbook while Ted watched, growing paler, too, by the second.

"You didn't…forget to pay the premium, did you?" he asked in a deceptively soft-sounding voice while his facial color began to reverse, going from white to red. When Melody nodded, her own green eyes huge and frightened, Leslie thought that Ted was about to explode.

"Don't worry about it!" she cried quickly. "I'll take care of the repairs. I have some money in the bank, and my credit's good. Don't give it another thought."

"I can't let you do that!" Ted's face was anguished.

"Of course you can. If I hadn't borrowed your car, this would never have happened before you discovered your—mistake." Leslie smiled brightly, trying to avert a family disaster. "Why, you can drive around New York for years without getting hit by an uninsured drunk at eleven in the morning."

"Repairs on Corvettes come pretty high," Ted said dubiously. "I'll tell you what, I'll pay you back as soon as I get another job lined up."

"Only half," Leslie insisted. "It wasn't such a bad stroke of luck for me. Mr. Brookens from the publishing house dropped in to see me a while ago, and they're going to do my book. I'll be getting a nice little advance, too." Of course, she thought wryly, she wouldn't receive any money until the book was published, but there was no point in telling Ted and Melody that.

"Congratulations! That's great," Ted said happily, and Leslie knew that she had won him over.

"Just let me know when you find out how much it's going to cost," she said.

Three days later Leslie sat at her desk by the window of her SoHo apartment, staring at the dollar figure she had just scribbled on a pad of paper. Ted hadn't been kidding. Repairs on Corvettes did come very high! Leslie sneezed, blew her nose and swore softly. A cold on top of everything else! She stared at her bank balance, back at the numbers on the paper and then very deliberately snapped the pencil in half and heaved it toward her door, the pieces striking it just as there was a knock.

"Who is it?" she barked.

"'Tis only I, your neighbor," said a tall blond woman, poking her head gingerly in the door and looking at the pieces of pencil lying on the floor. "Uh-oh. What happened? You run out of pottery to throw?"

"Hi, Susan, come on in. No, I've reformed. Pencils are easier to clean up. What brings you home at lunchtime? Did Mr. Pike run out of things for you to do?"

"Hah! Far from it. I've got to zip out to Kennedy airport and meet an important client a little later so I thought I'd change into a more smashing outfit, and while I was here, I figured I'd check to see how you're recovering from the accident, since I haven't seen you in a couple of days."

Leslie shrugged. "Pretty well. The stitches in my arm only wake me up a couple of times a night now, and my head's feeling fine again. Aside from the spring cold I've picked up, I thought I was doing great until my sister called a few minutes ago."

"What's wrong? The baby's not sick, is he?"

"No, he's fine."

Susan clucked sympathetically as Leslie explained the source of her problem, finishing with, "You don't happen to know of a bank that's an easy stickup, do you?"

Susan chuckled. "Not right offhand. That's a ghastly sum, all right. You're going to have to learn to curb those mad impulses of yours."

"I know." Leslie sighed and shook her head. "But it was the first really nice spring day, and I could just picture myself sweeping through the gates of that estate in a Corvette instead of a rented heap. I guess I should have remembered what the fortune-teller told me at that party at the United Nations last Christmas."

"You mean the one who told me I was going to meet 'zee tall, dark stranger' just before I met the president of Ghana?"

"That's the one," Leslie chuckled. "She told me I should curb 'zee impulsive nature' or I was going to be in very bad trouble sometime. Of course, my mother's been telling me that for years."

"You're not really in trouble, are you?" Susan asked, her fine brows knit in concern. "You aren't going to have to sell your Hasselblad to pay for that darned car, I hope."

"Goodness, no! I'll cope, somehow. If necessary I can get a bank loan, but if I can get a few extra jobs, I may not have to do that. Which reminds me, does your agency have any crumbs they could throw my way in the next few weeks? I'm going to be finishing up those pictures of the New York markets that I've been doing for *Produce Quarterly* this afternoon, weather permitting, and after that I don't have anything scheduled until my trip to El Salvador with the British writer at the end of the month."

Susan worked for an advertising agency that availed itself of Leslie's award-winning skills whenever she could be diverted from what she considered her real work, that of photographing the human side of newsworthy events around the world, whether they be wars or royal weddings. The award, which she had won for a picture of a little girl gazing awestruck at Prince Charles and Diana, the Princess of Wales, as they entered their coach after their wedding, occupied a place of honor on Leslie's wall, the framed original photograph above it. At Leslie's question, Susan's face was suddenly illuminated by a broad grin.

"As a matter of fact, I do," she said. "I didn't know quite how to approach you, knowing how you feel about Molly Primrose, but Mr. Pike told me to try to get you to do that fashion stint with her in St. Louis next week."

Leslie groaned. "I thought you had Clarence Quillen lined up for that. What happened?"

"He found out his lover's having an affair with some German baron and took off like a shot on the first Concorde. How about it? Mr. Pike will love you forever."

"I guess I can't afford to say no," Leslie said dryly. "But dear Miss Molly won't get the kid-gloved treatment from me that she would have from Clarence. She was named model of the year two years ago, not model of the century. Any of her regal temperament and I'll make her look twenty pounds fatter."

"Now, now," Susan teased. "Curb those impulses." She got to her feet and started for the door. "I'd better phone in the good news and get ready for my afternoon pickup." Then she stopped and turned back, her eyes bright. "Why didn't I remember this before! We still haven't found a winner in the Fling soft-drink promotion contest, which means that the ten thousand dollars is still up for grabs. Why don't you try finding us the Fling man? It would solve all of your financial problems with money to spare."

"Oh, come on, Susan! I can't do that sort of thing. Can't you just picture me sidling up to some handsome hunk—" Leslie stood and assumed a coy pose, furiously batting her long, rust-colored lashes over her green eyes "—and saying, 'Pardon me, sir. I'm Leslie Lyon, and I'm looking for the Fling man. No, no, I don't want to have a fling with you, you gorgeous thing.

Fling is a wonderful new soft drink we're promoting, and we need someone very special to represent it, someone any woman would love to have a fling with. You're so terribly handsome, and your muscles are so—so muscular. Won't you let me take your picture so you can become the latest sex symbol, and I can win a great big prize?' '' She grinned as Susan laughed uproariously.

"I'm not sure that approach would work with the kind of man we're looking for," Susan said as her laughter quieted.

"Oh? Well it's the only approach I can think of," Leslie replied. "I'm surprised no one's won the prize yet. Goodness knows there are a lot of muscle men around these days. Why doesn't someone just go and check out all the health clubs in the city?"

"From what I've seen, they have, but that's not the type we're looking for. We're looking for someone more...mature."

"Mature? Hmmm. Well, Ted's mature, and he's nice-looking, if not spectacular. That would certainly solve everyone's problems all at once."

Susan shook her head. "He'd be fine with me, but...well, this is supposed to be a big secret, but we've had word from on high. Mrs. Cliveden Phillips, the wife of the CEO of International Enterprises, which is the conglomerate that owns Superior Soft Drinks, passed the word down to our judges that what she would like to see is someone more along the lines of a reincarnation of Clark Gable. Rumor has it that she has all of his movies on tape and watches them over and over."

"Lots of luck to her," Leslie said dryly. "I wouldn't mind finding such a man, either. From all the stories

I've heard, Clark Gable not only looked terrific in the movies, but he was a pretty terrific man in real life.''

"Well, keep your eyes open," Susan said airily. "This may be your day for meeting 'zee tall, dark stranger.' ''

"Hah!" Leslie snorted, crinkling her nose so that its light sprinkling of freckles danced from side to side. "I've had them open for someone like that for years. And I've met plenty of tall, dark strangers—with the accent on 'strange.' Usually they try to convince you that going to bed on the first date is the best way to 'get acquainted,' but the last one I met spent three hours trying to convince me to become a vegetarian. Maybe I've just lost my sex appeal." She paused to sneeze violently into a hastily grabbed Kleenex. "With this cold I'd probably make a hit with Rudolph the Red-Nosed Reindeer.''

"I doubt if bosomy redheads have gone out of style," Susan said cheerfully. "You just haven't met your soul mate yet. Well, take care of yourself. You really shouldn't be going out this afternoon with that awful cold. It's so damp and chilly.''

"I'll bundle up," Leslie promised as she gingerly mopped her irritated nose. "Winter parka and wool slacks it is.''

"I BEG YOUR PARDON, young lady.''

The deep, impatient voice behind Leslie startled her. Her attention had been concentrated on the pictures she was taking of a man and a young boy unloading crates of lettuce from a semitrailer some distance down the loading dock at New York's mammoth Hunt's Point produce terminal. Drat! That shot would have been the best of the bunch, and it was spoiled. The way rain kept threatening she'd be lucky to get another one as good. She whirled around, frowning.

"Why don't you—" Her words deteriorated into a strangled sound as her gaze met a pair of dark eyes flashing impatiently beneath straight black brows. She continued to stare in disbelief at the familiar-looking, handsome face.

"Would you mind moving?"

"Oh! Yes. Sorry." Leslie jumped aside, suddenly aware that she was forcing the man to stand holding a heavy box of lemons.

"Thanks," the man said with a wry, humorous twist to his mouth, as if he were perfectly well aware of the effect his appearance had had on Leslie. He pushed past her and deposited the box on a pallet on a forklift, then turned to retrieve another box from his truck.

My God, it's him, Leslie thought, her heart beating fast and a strange, dreamlike sense overcoming her. The man did not look exactly like Mrs. Phillips's idol but close enough to be a member of the same family. He would be absolutely perfect for the Fling promotion, a sure prizewinner! He was a prizewinner in many ways already, Leslie thought as her eyes remained glued to the man's form. In spite of the coolness of the March day, the sleeves of his khaki-colored shirt were rolled up above his elbows, revealing strongly muscled arms. The fabric was taut across shoulders that could only be described as massive. Snugly fitted jeans showed that the rest of the man's physique left nothing to be desired, either.

What on earth do I do now? Leslie wondered, licking her lips nervously, her eyes following the man as he moved with an easy, arrogant grace between the back of his truck and the pile he was building for the forklift to

carry away. Visions of pictures of the man using the
promotional theme Have a Fling with Me alternated
with images of someone handing her a check for ten
thousand dollars. *Snap out of it, Leslie,* she told herself. *You've got to make a move. Think!*

But her feet remained rooted to the spot, her anxiety
increasing by the minute as her mind seemed unwilling
to function. She had not done any serious thinking
about how she might approach a man for the Fling
promotion, feeling that it was not her cup of tea at all,
but now she wished desperately that she had. She had a
strong intuition that, if she tried the simpering approach she had demonstrated to Susan, this man would
laugh in her face.

He continued to move back and forth from his truck
to the forklift, unloading the cargo of lemons and
shouting amiably to a rather unsavory-looking character he called Tony who was helping him. Apparently, he
was oblivious to Leslie's existence now that she was no
longer in his way. At the rate he was going, he would be
through with his job and out of the terminal before
Leslie had said a word. Where would he be going? she
wondered.

She noticed the man called Tony eyeing her with a
speculative leer and at last forced herself to look away
and make her feet move close enough so that she could
read the printing on the door of the truck. Buena Suerte
Farms, Brawley, California, the sign read in a casual
combination of languages. Good Luck Farms, Leslie
translated. Well, it would be *buena suerte* for both of
them if she could talk him into becoming the man who
represented Fling, his picture on posters all over the
country. Truck driving didn't pay all that well, she
knew. Still, she couldn't very well go up to him and say

"Hey, mister, how would you like to make a lot of money?" He would think she was either propositioning him or trying to involve him in something illegal. Maybe if she first approached him about being photographed for *Produce Quarterly*, that might break the ice. It wasn't a brilliant idea, but it was a start.

"I beg your pardon," Leslie said at last, getting herself in position to waylay the man after he had deposited a box of lemons on the latest pile. "I'm a photographer...."

The man stopped as Leslie planted herself in front of him.

"So I gathered," he said, looking pointedly at the cameras slung around Leslie's neck and giving her an amused smile, one eyebrow cocked upward.

Good Lord, but he's sexy, Leslie thought, feeling her knees quiver strangely. She had to suppress a reflexive desire to bat her eyelashes in response to his smile, no doubt something this handsome devil was quite used to. She managed instead what she hoped was a cool little smile in return.

"And," she went on as if he had not interrupted, "I am taking some pictures of men at work here at Hunt's Point for *Produce Quarterly*. Would it be all right with you if I take some shots of you and your friend doing your unloading?"

The man's smile faded, and his second eyebrow rose to join the first in a rueful expression as he shook his head.

"I'm afraid not," he replied. "I don't think it would be appropriate under the circumstances."

The man turned away again and left Leslie once more staring after him, dumbfounded. What kind of circumstances could possibly make it inappropriate for him to be photographed for a trade publication? She roused herself and pursued him to the back of his truck.

"What circumstances?" she demanded, coming up behind him. "I mean, it's not as if your picture were going to be spread all over some scandal sheet."

The man glanced back over his shoulder, the smile again creating deeply creased dimples in his cheeks.

"It's a long and complicated story, Miss—"

"Lyon," Leslie supplied. "Leslie Lyon."

"Well, little Miss Lyon, I am not really trying to make your job more difficult—"

"Duke, we've got some broken boxes here," called the man who was helping to unload.

"Coming, Tony," the man called Duke replied. He gave Leslie an apologetic and, Leslie thought, completely adorable wink. "Excuse me," he said, heading for the spot where Tony stood, deep in the recesses of the truck.

Leslie felt slightly dizzy. Whether it was from the strong antihistamine she had taken for her cold or from the wink, she wasn't sure. The man called Duke certainly had plenty of charm—and he knew how to use it. Duke. How absolutely appropriate his name was! He looked as if he were quite used to lording it over both men and women. Rather strange for someone who apparently drove a truck for a big California fruit grower. And how amazing that none of the movie scouts had discovered him. They had certainly missed a jewel.

She continued watching as Duke called the broken boxes to the attention of the person from the warehouse who was checking the load. Her mind came up with nothing but blanks as she tried to think of some way to approach Duke on the subject of the Fling promotional campaign. She almost giggled hysterically as she thought wildly of curtsying and saying in her best Eliza Doolittle accent "I say, yer lawdship, 'ow'd you like to 'av your picture took for some posters?" Her eyes were still sparkling with mirth when Duke stopped in front of her, his own eyes glittering with a warmth that Leslie analyzed as somewhere past friendly, on the way to seductive.

"Is there something else I can do for you, Miss Lyon?" he asked in a deep, slightly husky voice.

"Oh, yes!" Leslie blurted, then felt her cheeks grow warm as Duke's smile widened into a grin. The nerve of him, thinking she had meant... Not that a lot of women wouldn't be instantly ready to jump into bed with this overpoweringly masculine creature! But she certainly wasn't. Tightening her arms around herself until the still-sore stitches in her arm gave a twinge of pain, Leslie gathered her wits and said in stiffly starched tones, "There was something else I wanted to discuss with you. Perhaps when you've finished unloading, if you could spare a few minutes...?"

The quirky little half smile appeared again. "You make it sound very mysterious and enticing, Miss Lyon. Now, ordinarily, I would ask such an attractive young lady out to dinner, and we could discuss any number of things at length. But, unfortunately, very unfortunately, I have to be in Paterson, New Jersey, this afternoon to pick up a load and then start heading back to California. Perhaps next time I'm in town..."

"Duke Caldwell, telephone call for you in the manager's office," came a loud voice from some hidden speaker.

"Don't go away," said the man named Duke Caldwell, giving Leslie another of those intimate little winks before he vaulted gracefully down from the loading dock and headed toward the manager's office with more than a hint of swagger in his walk.

He thinks I'm coming on to him, Leslie thought crossly. *He really does have an inflated ego.* For all she knew, he had a nice little wife and family tucked away somewhere. But as blatant as his sexuality was, any wife would sleep poorly when he was on the road, wondering if he was really being faithful or had found someone to share his bed for the night. She lowered herself from the loading dock and started walking idly around Duke Caldwell's truck. The refrigerated trailer was a gleaming silver, the logo of Buena Suerte Farms, a huge horseshoe, emblazoned on both sides and on the back. The tractor that pulled the rig was iridescent blue, liberally splashed with chrome trim. It did have an oversize sleeper, a perfect place for a man like Duke Caldwell to—

"Cut it out, Leslie," she muttered, embarrassed by her mental meanderings. She was spending entirely too much time connecting Duke Caldwell with beds, and judging by his obvious effect on her hormone balance, that could be dangerous. Duke Caldwell did not look as if he would be shy about exploiting his powers.

Several large raindrops spattered the truck and Leslie's head simultaneously.

"Oh, no!" she cried, looking up in dismay at the dark clouds overhead. Where was the man? His phone call was taking forever! She thought momentarily of taking refuge in the now largely empty trailer, but a second thought quickly became more appealing. Why not wait for him in the cab of his truck? That would be a good place to talk to him, away from the hustle and interruptions of other people. If only it weren't locked. She climbed the steps and tried the door, which opened easily, gaining her access to the passenger's seat and shelter just as the rain began to pelt down in earnest.

"Whew! Just in time," she breathed, surveying the torrent from her lofty perch. She removed her cameras from around her neck and carefully wiped off the raindrops, then tucked the gear into her camera bag, waiting and watching for any sign of Duke Caldwell's return. When he had not appeared in fifteen minutes, she grew restless, the thought occurring to her that, if he wanted to be in Paterson this afternoon, he would have precious little time to talk to her before he left.

"Just long enough to tell me no, but he could think of something more interesting to do next time he's in town," Leslie muttered under her breath, although why she knew his immediate response would be no she was not sure. Whether she could talk him into a yes, given enough time, was another question. But how could she get enough time? Maybe he would let her ride along with him for a ways. No, probably not, at least not for the purpose she had in mind.

Leslie fidgeted in her seat, trying to think of some way around her problem and at the same time taking in the interior of the truck cab, its wide dashboard covered with numerous inscrutable gauges, the walls and ceiling padded with a quilted leatherlike material in a deep blue color. A matching heavy plastic fabric covered the wall separating the driving compartment from the sleeper, a zippered opening serving as a doorway. She pushed the zipper partway open and peered into the sleeper. The light was dim from a tiny round window high up on one wall above the bunk, but she could see that, between the door and the large double bunk at the back, adorned with lumpy piles of bedclothes, there was a space containing assorted built-in shelves and drawers for storage.

Looks as if you could just about live in there, she thought, withdrawing her head from the opening. Then another thought occurred to her, and she first smiled to herself and then chuckled with delight. What if she hid in there until Duke was on the highway to Paterson? He couldn't throw her out on the interstate, and he would have to pay attention to his driving so he wouldn't be able to assault her in any way, sexual or otherwise. Of course, she'd have to be careful how she made her entrance so that she didn't scare the poor man to death. But . . . sure, why not? She didn't have anything pressing to do for the rest of the day. She already had enough pictures of the terminal, and she had enough money to take a bus back from Paterson. Of course, if anyone had seen her get into the truck, they might give her away, but the way everyone had scattered when it started to pour rain, she doubted she'd been noticed.

Then let's do it! she encouraged herself mentally, reaching for the zipper and quickly sliding through the opening and refastening it. She felt very large and conspicuous in the small space. What if Duke looked in there before he started out? She'd better hide. In seconds she tucked her camera bag under the bunk and lay down, rearranging what turned out to be a sleeping bag over herself and hoping that the bed did not look much lumpier than it had before. Only moments later she heard the truck door open and close and the creaking of the seat as someone sat down. Leslie held her breath, then her heart sank as she heard the zipper moving. She froze, still barely breathing. Suddenly something heavy landed with a thump on her derrière, and she flinched a little, involuntarily. But when nothing happened and she heard the sound of the zipper being refastened, she began to breathe again.

He didn't look, Leslie thought triumphantly, her heart racing now. So far, so good. Then her stomach tightened in apprehension at the sound of the other door opening. It hadn't occurred to her that Duke might have someone with him. The apprehension changed to a sickly knot as she recognized Tony's guttural voice.

"I really appreciate your giving me a ride to Paterson, Duke. I haven't seen my sister in two months."

"Happy to oblige you, Tony," the deep, slightly husky voice of Duke Caldwell replied as the truck started to move. "Glad to have the company. Which reminds me, I wonder what became of the pretty little redhead? She said she wanted to talk to me."

"Oh-ho! So you were hoping for a lot better company than me," Tony said with a suggestive guffaw that sent chills down Leslie's spine. The throaty chuckle from Duke Caldwell that followed Tony's remark did nothing to calm her fears. What kind of a mess had she gotten herself into now! And how on earth was she going to get out of it?

CHAPTER TWO

DRAT! LESLIE THOUGHT, trying to find a more comfortable position for her sore arm and aching head. Twenty-seven years of age was a little old to be recalling her mother's frequent scolding, "You should have thought of that before, dear." Was she doomed forever to rush headlong into situations any sensible person would have avoided? She probably should have thought twice about borrowing Ted and Melody's expensive car, knowing, as she did, the vagaries of New York traffic and Melody's erratic bookkeeping. And she definitely should have thought three or four times about this little caper! She wasn't that desperate for the money. And, if worse came to worst, facing a bank-loan officer was a lot less intimidating than two macho-type men, bent on proving their masculinity!

But ten thousand dollars would solve her problem nicely...not to mention the fun of winning itself... and it hadn't sounded like such a bad plan...at first. Even now, in the best possible scenario—after Tony had gone and if she still hadn't been discovered—she might be able to sneak out and then suddenly appear as if from out of nowhere and have that conversation with Duke Caldwell after all. He would be so perfect for the job. But would he take it? Well, why not? Truckers weren't rich, and it would make him a pretty penny, could even lead to other advertising jobs. But he hadn't wanted his picture even in *Produce Quarterly*. That was certainly strange. Why would that be? A complicated story? Curious... *He* was curious. Handsome, articulate... sexy. Very sexy. And she was hiding in his bed. Maybe she should wonder why that was. And maybe she shouldn't.

Stop dithering and think! Leslie told herself severely, scrunching her eyes in the dark as if to ward off evil images, and trying to take some deep, even breaths. She was glad for the noise of the traffic and the endless shifting of the truck's sixteen gears, for she was sure that otherwise the men would have been able to hear the pounding of her heart.

Was there any chance that she could stick her head out from the sleeper and state her business fast and convincingly enough to overcome any other ideas they might have? Leslie thought about that for a moment and then shook her head. The very nature of her "business" implied that she thought that Duke was handsome and sexy, and Tony looked like the type who would concentrate on that aspect of her offer to the exclusion of anything else. Besides, two men out to impress each other with their masculinity were far more dangerous than one, especially when the one appeared about a hundred times more gentlemanly than the other. Duke alone, she thought, might be a pretty safe bet, although she might be wrong about that, as stupid as she'd been lately. But she was definitely not going to take on the two of them.

There was no way she could get out of the moving truck. She would just have to bide her time until she could sneak away without the two men seeing her. That would, of course, mean the end of any chance she had to get Duke Caldwell to be the Fling man, unless she

could track him down in California after she finished
the job in St. Louis. No, that wouldn't be practical. A
trip like that could eat up all the profit from her fashion work, and she'd still wind up with nothing. Darn!

Suddenly a violent sneeze overcame Leslie. Oh, no!
Her antihistamine was wearing off. She held her breath,
expecting someone to peer into the sleeper at any moment, then realized suddenly that they couldn't have
heard her above the blaring country-and-western music on the radio. Maybe she could risk finding her bottle of pills in her camera bag. Carefully she uncovered
her head and looked around, able to see a lot more
clearly in the dim light after having been in the dark for
so long. She could see that the object that had hit her on
the bottom was a bag of apples. Against the forward
wall she saw, to her surprise, a small refrigerator tucked
under a counter, which even had a washbasin. The
compartment really was almost like a camping trailer.
Stealthily she reached under the bunk and found her
camera bag, opened it and felt for the bottle. In moments she had a pill in her hand. Could she swallow it
without any water? It was quite large.

All I need is to start choking on the darn thing, Leslie thought, frowning. She eyed the little refrigerator
speculatively. Maybe there was something to drink in
there that she could get without making too much noise.
She crept off the bunk onto the floor and opened the
door. Oh, good. There was a bottle of some kind of
fruit drink. Carefully she twisted off the lid and sniffed.
It smelled like apricots, and a quick taste affirmed what
her stuffy nose had told her. In fact, it was especially
delicious, and she was very thirsty.

"Mmmm, good," Leslie murmured when she had
downed half the bottle. It had a pleasantly relaxing ef-

fect on her, too. She would have to ask Duke what brand of juice it was. Yes, she would ask him. She definitely was not going to give up on him after coming this far. As soon as he got rid of Tony, she'd let him know she was here. In the meantime, why not take a little nap?

IT WAS VERY QUIET, the diesel silent, the feeling of motion gone. Leslie opened her eyes, wondering at first why it was so dark and then remembering with a panicky start where she was. Her head felt fuzzy and achy. Darn this cold, she thought as she cautiously lifted the edge of the sleeping bag and peeked out. She was alone. It was still dimly lighted in the sleeping compartment. Outside she could hear voices and the sudden roar of another truck nearby. Were they in Paterson already? Had Tony gone?

Carefully Leslie crept near the little round window, got up on her knees and peered out. They were at a truck stop, parked by the diesel-fuel pumps. The brilliant fluorescent lights illuminating the large parking and restaurant areas were as bright as day, which was obviously over. Good heavens, where were they? How long had she slept? She could see Duke through the glass doors of the station, paying his bill. Tony was nowhere in sight. She had better make up her mind to either put in her appearance or get out of here altogether—and fast!

Swiftly she grabbed her camera bag, reached for the compartment door's zipper, then dropped her hand at the sound of the driver's door opening. Good Lord! Duke was back already! And he was talking to someone outside. Was Tony still with him? Had he, perhaps, just dropped him off? Chewing her lip anxiously,

Leslie strained to hear the conversation. No, it wasn't Tony's gruff voice, but it wasn't a very pleasant-sounding one, either, and the words were positively chilling.

"Aw, come on, Duke, whatcha hiding the little dolly for? I seen her get in your truck way back at Hunt's Point. You gonna keep her all to yourself all the way to California?"

Before slamming his door vehemently, Duke snarled back, "There is no little dolly in my truck. Now get your filthy hands off it before I knock them off." And with a roar that sounded like a continuation of his snarl, he started the mighty diesel engine and immediately set the truck in motion again.

Leslie sank back down on the edge of the bunk with a groan that would have been audible if Duke had not suddenly switched on his radio full blast to a country-and-western station. He had sounded absolutely furious at the suggestion that she might be in his truck. He had to be married, she decided, and very devotedly so, his earlier contrary indication only a game, the kind of thing men did to keep up their macho image.

I'm in for it now, she thought gloomily. *I'd better hope he throws me out of the truck when it's stopped instead of moving.* The only question was whether to stick her head into the cab and risk scaring him into a wreck or let him discover her and have a heart attack then.

The question was decided for her when the truck slowed suddenly, took a sharp curve and then came to a stop. Leslie was scrambling toward the tiny window when she was startled by a light coming on in the sleeper. She froze and looked toward the doorway, which opened to admit Duke Caldwell, his gleaming dark eyes fixed on hers as if he were not even slightly surprised by her presence, as if he were intent on only one purpose. Without saying a word, he launched himself across the bunk, grabbed her roughly, flattened her against the bunk and clamped his hand tightly across her mouth. He stared at her intently, his eyes glittering coldly.

"Strange," he growled from between clenched teeth, "you don't look the part. Perhaps a little test is in order." With that he slid his hand away, covering Leslie's mouth firmly with his own.

Test? Leslie thought vaguely, still too shocked and frightened to think clearly. What kind of test was this? She tried to wriggle free, but Duke was far too heavy, her feeble movements useless. She tried pounding on his back with her fists, but the action was ineffectual, the movement of Duke's mouth against hers too insistent to ignore. The lashing of his tongue against her lips as he forced them apart was too sensually warm and moist to deny.

With a weak little moan Leslie opened her mouth to the onslaught. Duke's tongue darted inside, teasing and probing. Leslie responded, the heat of the interchange sending waves of desire coursing through her in spite of her fear. Their swollen lips slid back and forth with increasing pressure, a dizzying escalation that left Leslie breathless, clutching at Duke's back. She felt as if she were sinking into a delicious fog, her only desire to hold this man even closer, until . . .

Good heavens! Like a jolt of electricity, the shock of what she was doing and where it was leading chilled Leslie to the bone. Had she lost her mind? With a desperate wrenching movement she jerked her head back, simultaneously clamping her teeth down on Duke's lower lip.

He gave a muffled curse and raised his head, one hand taking a painful grip on her hair while the other swiftly covered her mouth again.

"Why, Miss Lyon," he snarled sarcastically, "didn't they tell you to be more cooperative? And just when you were doing so well, too."

Leslie tried to struggle, but Duke's grip on her hair was too painful, and his body still had her firmly pinned to the bunk. She felt as if she were living in a nightmare. Who was he talking about? Who did he think had told her—what? Why did he think she was here? His next statements did nothing but add to her confusion.

"You'll find it much less painful if you stop squirming," he said, his eyes glittering coldly as he looked down at Leslie, his mouth curved downward in disgust. "I wondered why you were here—oh yes, I knew it all along—but when Callahan asked about you, it suddenly all fell into place. What were you supposed to do? Spend the night with me, sneak a few pictures of us in bed together while I slept and then join Callahan the first chance you got the next morning? Well I've got news for you, young lady. You're going to stay right here until you're ready to sign a statement about who hired you and how much they're paying you for this little job. So it's up to you how long you want to be my *guest*. Meanwhile, I think I'll just lock your cameras away to make sure you aren't tempted to carry out your mission. Where are they? And don't try to scream when I take my hand away. I'll see that you regret it if you do."

Very carefully Duke raised his hand a few inches above Leslie's mouth. "Well?" he said.

Leslie's lips felt as dry as a desert, and she could not tell whether it was Duke's weight or sheer fear that made it hard for her to breathe. Something was terribly wrong, and she had no idea what it was.

"I—I don't know what you're talking about," she croaked.

There was no softening in Duke's expression as he snorted in disgust, "That was very good. Almost worthy of a CIA agent. Did they also tell you that, if you blew your cover, they would disavow any knowledge of you?" He gave Leslie's hair an extra, painful jerk.

Like a cornered animal, Leslie felt her fear suddenly change to a white-hot anger that blotted out any pain. With a strength she didn't know she possessed, she suddenly jerked and pushed, almost flinging Duke Caldwell off the bunk.

"Get off me and stay off! I have no idea what your insane accusations are about. I thought I might have a job for you, but I no longer want anything to do with you! Now get out of my way. I'm leaving." She tried to push past him, but he easily stayed her, grasping her upper arms and again pushing her back against the bunk, his head bending close to hers, his voice silky but his eyes a steely dark blend of black and brown.

"My, my, such a hot-tempered little redhead. Nice try. I don't blame you for wanting out, now that you can see you won't be collecting anything for a successful mission. How much were they going to pay you for trapping me?" One eyebrow slanted upward as Leslie glared silently at him. He shook her none too gently. "Come on, Miss Lyon. The longer you stall, the more painful this is going to be—for both of us. I have no more desire to keep you here than you have to stay."

"No one was going to pay me anything," she snapped. "I had hoped to win a prize for finding someone to represent a new soft drink called Fling. I was obviously mistaken in thinking that you might do." Her eyes widened as Duke threw back his head and laughed. *The man is crazy!* she thought. *None of his responses are connected to reality at all.*

"Whoever told you to use that story certainly got their wires crossed," he said, shaking his head and still grinning as if something were extremely amusing. "But I'm not surprised. Half of old Clive Phillips's political henchmen have no idea how many pies International Enterprises have their fingers in. If they did, they'd know that I'm the last man on earth that Clive would hire for his poster boy." His eyes narrowed as he surveyed Leslie's face thoughtfully. "Just how much did they tell you, I wonder? Or did you have no idea at all what you were getting into?"

He could say that again, Leslie thought, bewildered. She had apparently blundered into some intrigue involving powerful Cliveden Phillips and this truck driver, whose flirtatious interest in her on the dock at Hunt's Point had turned into something more like a tiger's interest in a helpless victim. Wasn't there anything she could say to convince him she was not some kind of Mata Hari? If she could not, there was no telling what he might do. She licked her lips nervously.

"Really, Mr. Caldwell," she said, trying for a normal voice but instead sounding pitifully strained. "I have no idea what you are talking about."

There was another disbelieving snort from Duke Caldwell.

"You know my name," he said as if that proved she was lying.

Leslie scowled. "They called it over the loudspeaker at the terminal," she said coldly. "I assumed since you went to take the call that that was your name."

Duke Caldwell sighed as though his patience were nearly exhausted.

"You are most annoyingly stubborn, Miss Lyon. Perhaps it would be more productive if we went back to our earlier activity." He bent his head even closer, his lips curving into a devilish smile as Leslie twisted her head away. "Why fight it, Miss Lyon? You know you were really beginning to enjoy my kiss." He placed his lips against the corner of Leslie's mouth very softly, nibbling teasingly. "You might as well get something out of this disaster," he whispered.

"No!" Leslie grated, her jaws clenched, as she tried to writhe out of his tight hold. The last thing in the world she wanted was her body to betray her again with this madman. She could feel the heat of his lips, feel her skin respond as if a current were being passed between them. "No, don't," she growled as he pursued her mouth with insistent pressure. As she tried to fight free, he tightened his grip on her arms, and she let out a little cry of pain.

"Darn you!" she cried. "You've torn one of my stitches. Let go of me!"

"What stitches?" Duke raised his head, scowling suspiciously. "Did your last boyfriend get a little too rough?" Nevertheless, he relinquished his grip on Leslie's arms and permitted her to sit up.

"You rotten creep, you would think something like that," Leslie snarled, feeling inside her jacket. "You are the most loathsome, disgusting person I have ever met. It so happens that I was in an automobile accident."

"Let me see," Duke commanded.

"I will not," Leslie snapped back. She was not about to take off her sweater in front of this maniac.

"Miss Lyon, as I have pointed out before, you will find life much simpler if you do as I tell you. Now take off your jacket, or I will take it off for you."

Leslie stared at him defiantly but inwardly realized the hopelessness of her refusal. He would probably tear her jacket to shreds if she continued to refuse. With a grimace she peeled back her left jacket sleeve and pushed up her sweater to show him the bandage, which now had a large stain showing through it. Duke looked at it closely.

"All right, I believe you. Take off your sweater so I can see how much damage there is. I've got some first-aid supplies. We can at least give you a clean bandage." When Leslie didn't make a move, he reached for the bottom of her sweater.

"Hands off!" Leslie attempted to push his hand away, and when he persisted, she swung wildly at his face, only to have her hand caught in a vicelike grip.

"You little hellion," he said calmly. "Don't you ever learn? But then, why should I expect anything else from a Lyon?" While saying so he was easily controlling Leslie's hands and at the same time lifting one side of her sweater. "Pull your arm out," he ordered.

"I've had that line used on me so many times it's sickening," Leslie grumbled as she complied. "That and the nonsense about all redheads being hot-tempered."

Duke chuckled. "I'll try to be more original in the future. Now hold very still, if you can."

While Leslie watched silently, he carefully removed her bandage, frowning as he saw the long, deep cut. "That is a nasty one," he remarked. "What happened?" He got up and retrieved a box from a wall cabinet, raising his eyebrows questioningly at Leslie, who had not replied.

"A drunk ran a stop sign and hit my car broadside," she answered tightly. "Some glass cut my arm." There was no point in mentioning that it was a borrowed car. This sadistic monster would probably make some horrible misinterpretation about that, too.

"Do much damage to your car?" Duke asked as he took out a bottle of alcohol and proceeded to clean the wound gently. When Leslie sucked in a sudden breath as alcohol stung the reopened part of the cut, he looked up, his eyes now warm and concerned. "Sorry," he said softly.

"That's okay," Leslie said, biting her lip and watching Duke's fingers at work. Good Lord, what a cruel deception it was that he could look so gentle at will. How many women must have been led astray only to discover his darker side. Maybe even some poor soul who called herself his wife.

"There," Duke said moments later. "It doesn't look too bad. I think a butterfly bandage will repair the damage." He looked up at Leslie. "Your car?" he repeated, cocking that eyebrow again.

"A disaster," Leslie answered, thinking grimly that, if it hadn't been for that fiasco, she wouldn't be in this mess now. The fates certainly hadn't been in her corner lately.

"Was the driver insured?" Duke was carefully applying a small butterfly bandage to the part of the wound that was still bleeding slightly.

"No." Leslie could feel the next question coming as if she knew that Duke could read her mind.

"Were you?"

"I don't think that's any of your business," she replied.

"Oh, I think it is. It might explain why you were willing to try anything to make some extra money. Cars don't come cheap these days, and I suppose that a photographer does need a car." He put a large gauze square over Leslie's wound and carefully taped it down, looking up at her as he finished. "I'm right, aren't I?"

Leslie sighed. "Only partly, but I'm not going to bother to explain it to you because you wouldn't believe me, anyway."

"Try me," Duke commanded as he replaced the first-aid box and returned to sit on the edge of the bunk, his handsome face serious and a little less threatening. "Tell me where I'm wrong."

Eyeing him suspiciously, Leslie pulled her sweater back on. "Just about everywhere," she said. "It wasn't actually my car, and, no, I don't need one since I travel all over the world, not just around New York and it isn't practical to pay to keep a car I'd hardly ever use. I borrowed it from my sister and her husband. My sister's just had a baby recently, and what with all the confusion, she forgot to pay the insurance premium. Naturally, since I borrowed the car, and it wouldn't have been damaged if I hadn't, I offered to pay for the repairs. I did think the Fling contest would be a good way to get some extra money, but I did not enter into any conspiracy against you. I picked you because I thought you looked right for the job, and I figured a truck driver could use the money, too. I planned to talk to you on the way to Paterson and go back to New York from there, but when I found out Tony was along, I decided to wait until he left. Then I fell asleep. I don't know why I slept so long. It must have been the antihistamine I took, or maybe there was some kind of drug in that stuff I got out of your refrigerator. Anyway, I'm even sorrier than you are that I'm here, and there is nothing I'd like more than to get out of here and never set eyes on you again."

She frowned as Duke leaned over and opened the little refrigerator, pulled out the bottle and then uttered an expletive, shaking his head at Leslie, a wry smile on his face.

"Is that what you drank?" As Leslie nodded, he chuckled. "No wonder you slept. This is about half Southern Comfort." He replaced the bottle, then leaned his chin on his hand and stared thoughtfully at Leslie. "That's an interesting story, but certain parts of it don't add up, especially when I recall that you were supposedly taking pictures for the *Produce Quarterly* back there at Hunt's Point."

"What on earth does that have to do with anything?" Leslie cried, feeling frustration beginning to grip her again just when she'd thought she had at last made some headway against Duke Caldwell's wild fantasy.

"Why, Miss Lyon, if you really had anything to do with *Produce Quarterly*, you would have noticed that I am one of the West Coast editors. Not only that, you would doubtless know that Buena Suerte is one of the largest farms in the Imperial Valley, and I am not a truck driver for them."

"Wh-what are you, then?" Leslie asked, a sinking feeling hitting her already knotted stomach. If only she'd read the masthead in that blasted journal instead of just studying the pictures, she might not be in this mess now!

"Well, you see, Miss Lyon," Duke said with a grin and an arrogant toss of his black hair, "I *own* Buena Suerte Farms. I drive a truck now and then just to get out from behind my desk and have some time to think. Apparently this trip was very ill-advised, however. I hadn't counted on Clive Phillips's being this desperate, but I might have guessed after he offered one of my more attractive women friends a bundle to set me up for some risqué pictures at a sleazy motel. You do know who Cliveden Phillips is, hmmm?" He tilted a black eyebrow toward Leslie, who was staring at him in disbelief.

With an inward groan Leslie nodded. Yes, she knew of the man, all right, but certainly not for the reason Duke Caldwell thought, as someone who was supposedly paying her to be some kind of temptress. At least part of the picture was beginning to take shape. There was some kind of vendetta between the two rich and powerful men, and Cliveden Phillips's purposes could be served by having Duke Caldwell made to look as if he took a woman along on this trip for immoral purposes. But why?

"Would you mind telling me what this is all about?" she asked. "I know who Mr. Phillips is, and now I know who you are, but I really have no idea how I'm supposed to be involved."

Duke Caldwell shook his head. "You really are incredible. I suppose a tiny little thing like you with those big eyes is used to being able to pull the wool over men's eyes with that sweetly innocent look. Well, it's just not going to work with me. I'm sure even someone as desperate for the money as you must be must have asked a few questions about the job. Now tomorrow I'll be glad to go into the details of our feud and why the possibility of my being elected representative of the district in which Clive's corporation has several thousand acres of land has him ready to try anything to prevent it. But it's getting very late, and I have several full days of driving ahead of me. So if you'll just hand me your camera case, I'll lock it up, and we can get some sleep.''

"This is ridiculous," Leslie snapped, glaring as Duke took the camera bag from her and put it into a cabinet with a padlock, which he firmly closed. "Not only that, but you're going to be in a lot of trouble for this. I'll see that you're brought up on kidnapping charges. I can't stay here all night, much less for any longer. I haven't eaten, and I have other needs that can't be taken care of in here. Now either let me out of here or, by God, I will start to scream, and I'll scream until one of us gives up or I'm dead." She struggled to her feet in the small space and stood glaring at Duke, who was towering above her. "I really mean it," she warned. "You won't be able to sleep for a moment, and don't threaten to bind and gag me because, if you do that and I can't breathe with this cold, you'll find yourself with a murder charge." She felt rage begin to boil inside her again when Duke chuckled as if she were an imbecilic child. "Stop that!" she cried, stomping her foot down on one of his.

"Ouch!" Duke cried out but did not seem to be in much pain, for he was still grinning. "I knew you'd be trouble from the minute I set eyes on you," he said. "I should have taken you to the manager's office and had him keep you there. Now I will take you out in a moment. We're at a rest area along the interstate in western Pennsylvania, and you'll be able to use the rest room—with me waiting outside. You can do that this time because we're out in the country, with not a soul around to see. I can't permit it during the day, though, because I fully expect old Spike Callahan to start following me tomorrow when you don't appear on the scene as he's expecting. So during the day you can use the chemical toilet in here. As far as food goes, help yourself to anything in the cupboards or refrigerator. There's plenty of sandwich material, and I'll get more as we go along. There are quite a few magazines, too, so you can entertain yourself. Just stay away from the window. If you should by any chance succeed in signaling to Callahan, I'll have to turn you over to him, and I doubt if he'd be very happy to see you without those pictures you're supposed to get. He's probably in this for the money, too, so if I were you, I'd avoid that at all costs. I've heard Callahan gets pretty brutal.''

"I don't know any Callahan," Leslie said from between clenched teeth. She felt like remarking that Duke Caldwell was not on her list of men she would like to spend any time with, either, but thought better of it. There was no point in irritating him any further, when she was condemned to spend the night with him in that little sleeper. One thing was for sure. She wouldn't be sleeping.

Duke led the way out of the truck, helping Leslie down the steps in an almost gentlemanly fashion. The night air was icily crisp. The neat highway rest area was brightly lighted but, as Duke had said, totally deserted except for them. Leslie trudged toward the small building, her hands thrust deep in her jacket pockets. Suddenly she became aware of something small and cylindrical in her left pocket. An indelible marker that she used to mark film rolls! Maybe she could scrawl a message on the wall.

As if again reading her mind, Duke said warningly, "I hope you aren't planning on trying to leave some kind of message with a lipstick or something. If you are, forget it because I plan to frisk you before you go inside."

"I wouldn't think of it," Leslie replied as she desperately maneuvered the little marker with her fingers, trying to poke it up her sleeve. Just as they got to the door, she succeeded.

"All right, hands out of your pockets," Duke ordered, turning Leslie to face him.

Leslie complied, keeping her face carefully blank as he felt deep inside her jacket pockets and then did an entirely too-thorough job on the pockets of her slacks.

"What's this?" He pulled a small nail file from her back pocket and smiled grimly. "That would have done a nice job of scratching, wouldn't it?" He pocketed the file. "All right, go on."

"I'm surprised you aren't coming with me," Leslie said coldly, quickly turning her back to hide the triumphant look on her face. She could write a message now, and even if Duke chose to come into the ladies' rest room and check after she was through, there would be little he could do about it. The marker, she knew, could not be washed off or erased.

Once safely inside a booth, she hurriedly scrawled with shaking fingers:

Help! I'm being held captive in a Buena Suerte Farms truck, heading west. This is no joke! Please call the police!

She signed her name and added the date, feeling a strong sense of relief sweep over her. Surely someone would see the message within the next twenty-four hours. And wouldn't Duke Caldwell get the surprise of his life when a state trooper pulled him over and told him he was under arrest!

Leslie tossed the marker away with the paper towels after she had washed her hands, figuring that, if Duke was to find it later, he might suspect something. She did so want those troopers to be a real surprise. She arranged her face in a sullen pout and went to the door just as Duke called out to her.

"Hurry up!"

"Relax, I'm here," she snapped as she came through the door. "There aren't any windows in there to climb out of." She flicked a glance up at Duke from beneath her long lashes and then looked quickly away again. He had reverted to his charming side, his eyes appearing to be full of some kind of magical sparks.

He's nothing but a sneaky, lecherous devil. He must have decided to see if he couldn't promote something for the rest of the night, Leslie thought, a little shiver of fear going through her at the thought of what he could easily do if he decided not to bother with any strategy except force.

When they were back in the truck, Duke said, "I'm going to undress and then put on an old warm-up suit that I use for pajamas. You can watch or not, as you prefer."

"Thanks, but I'll pass," Leslie said coldly, turning to sit cross-legged on the bunk, her back to him, trying to ignore his deep chuckle at her reply. She had been right; he was going to try to be as seductive as possible. Well, it was wasted on her, although she did find it disturbing to think of him standing behind her naked. And why not? For all she knew, he was stripping for action.

"You could use one of my flannel shirts for a night-gown," Duke suggested amid the sounds of his clothing being removed.

"I don't plan to sleep," Leslie retorted. Especially not with him, in what was just one large double sleeping bag!

"Suit yourself, but it's going to be a long night."

"I had a long nap," Leslie reminded him.

"Ah, yes, my Southern Comfort. I'm surprised you don't have a hangover. You must drink quite a lot."

"I do not!" Leslie cried, jerking her head around, enraged by this latest slur on her character. She was just in time to catch Duke inserting one foot into his pajama bottoms and quickly turned her back, her cheeks burning. "My God, but you're slow at that," she snarled to cover her embarrassment, "and I am not a lush. It's just that I feel so rotten with everything that's happened and with this awful cold that I couldn't tell if I did have a hangover." She heard Duke sigh heavily.

"I'm sorry," he said then, his voice velvety soft. "Poor little thing, I'll bet it has been a rough day for you. Are you hungry?" As Leslie did not reply, her guard having instantly gone up at the gentleness in his voice, he added, "You can turn around. I'm decent now."

Leslie turned gingerly around and put her feet on the floor, trying to keep her eyes from being drawn to the sight of Duke Caldwell standing there in a soft gray warm-up suit that draped gracefully over his massive frame.

"I suppose I'm hungry, but I'm not sure I can eat," she muttered, staring in morbid fascination at the huge bare feet on the floor directly in front of her.

"How about a glass of milk, or maybe some juice? You should try to get a little something down. It's feed a cold, isn't it?"

Velvet would have grated in comparison to that voice, Leslie thought, digging her fingernails into her palms. The implied sympathy was getting to her where she was weakest, making her feel almost like crying. She was not going to do that, no matter what.

"Milk, I guess," she answered, flinching as a large hand cupped her chin and lifted her face. She knew her eyes had a suspicious hint of moisture in them, and she clenched her jaws and tried to glare back defiantly at Duke. He bent toward her, looking her face over intently, then stared into her eyes for a few seconds, his expression unreadable. When he had not released her face after what seemed an eternity, Leslie jerked her chin away.

"I'd prefer you didn't touch me," she snapped, trying to slow her rapid breathing.

Duke shook his head. "I think you're extremely ambivalent, as am I." He appeared to mentally shift gears as he straightened, turned and got out a carton of milk. "How about a peanut butter sandwich to go with this?" he suggested as he handed Leslie a glass. "They usually aren't hard to digest."

"Okay," she agreed, wondering why Duke Caldwell was suddenly so concerned for her well-being. Probably he was afraid he might be inconvenienced by having a corpse on his hands, she decided as she downed the milk silently, watching him preparing her sandwich with quick, economical movements. When he had finished, he took her empty glass, handed her the sandwich and sat down on the bunk beside her, munching on his own as he watched her eat.

"Must you stare at me?" Leslie asked irritably. "I feel enough like a caged monkey as it is."

"I can't help it. You're very pretty. I wonder what might have happened if we'd met under different circumstances."

Leslie flicked a quick glance at him and then returned her attention to the last of her sandwich.

"Absolutely nothing," she said tightly. "You're not my type." That same maddening chuckle greeted her remark, and she turned to scowl at Duke Caldwell. "You think you're every woman's type, don't you?"

"Not quite," he replied, still chuckling. "Now if you're finished, let's get some sleep. Just get into the sleeping bag and scoot on over."

"I will not!" Leslie cried, jumping to her feet and glaring down at Duke. "You get in the sleeping bag. I am going to stay right here, sitting on the edge of the bunk, all night."

Duke shook his head. "Oh, no. If you insist on staying out in the cold and freezing your pretty self, you're going to do it on the far side of the bunk. I don't want you getting up in the night and using some kind of abracadabra on that padlock to get at your cameras. For all I know, you're as skillful at that kind of thing as you are at driving men crazy with those big, innocent green eyes." He stood up and placed a hand on Leslie's back. "Go on, scoot across," he said, giving her a small push.

"Stop that," Leslie said crossly, pushing his arm away with her elbow and glaring up at him as she got to her knees and began crawling across the bunk. She got to the far side and turned to sit down, leaning against the side of the compartment and watching as Duke turned off the light. The enclosure was plunged into almost total darkness. She felt the bunk sag, and then a pillow was thrust into her lap.

"Here, at least try to get comfortable," Duke said, "and if you feel like sleeping, just lie down and get under the edge of the sleeping bag. There's no point in freezing, especially with that cold you've got."

"I'm overwhelmed by your concern," Leslie growled in reply, punching the pillow and putting it behind her. "I hope you have nightmares." She gasped as Duke suddenly leaned over her, his face so close that she could feel his warm breath and see the gleam of his white teeth as he smiled.

"Miss Lyon— I guess maybe we're familiar enough to be on a first-name basis now, aren't we? Leslie, I plan to sleep very well, and I hope that you do the same. Perhaps by tomorrow you'll be able to think more clearly, and we can get this whole sordid mess behind us. Who knows? I might even find it in my heart to forgive you if you agree to give a nice honest description of everything that led up to your being here. Think about that. It would be worth it."

Before Leslie could reply, his lips found hers, softly warm and gentle but persistent until, as if pulled by a magnet, her face tipped toward his and she kissed him back. An intoxicating warmth spread through her tired, aching body and left her feeling dizzy when he pulled his head back again and said huskily, "I think you see what I mean. Good night."

CHAPTER THREE

WHEN LESLIE WOKE, it was to daylight, the feeling of motion and the throbbing of the heavy diesel engine. Instead of being propped in the corner, she was stretched out comfortably beneath the thick, warm sleeping bag.

I wonder when that happened? she thought sleepily, turning on her side and staring toward the closed door to the driver's compartment. She had tried to stay awake and think through her problem, she could remember that, and she could also vaguely remember that her mind had not wanted to function, had wandered in a disordered, dreamlike state through the events of the day until she had closed her eyes and let sleep take her away from the terrors and turmoil.

Maybe I'll be able to do better this morning, she thought, yawning and pushing herself to a sitting position and running her fingers through her hair. *Lord, I must look a mess.* At that notion she smiled wryly to herself. Was she actually concerned about how she looked in Duke Caldwell's presence? That would certainly be a turnabout. Perhaps she was already beginning to suffer from the psychological adaptation that led captives to become admirers of their captors. If so, she would nip it in the bud. Duke might be physically attractive to her, but there was nothing else to recommend the man. Nothing at all. Besides—she smiled a smile of pleasure this time—she was not going to be his captive for much longer.

Any moment now she might expect to hear a siren from a police car, ordering the arrogant and erroneous Duke Caldwell to the side of the road. Then he would be in for some real fun, trying to explain why he had held her captive at all. Not only that—Leslie smiled again as she remembered the one intelligent thought she'd had before drifting off to sleep—but the very first thing she was going to do when she got to a telephone was to call Loren Barstow and initiate a suit that would cost Mr. Buena Suerte Farms one heck of a lot of lemons. Yes, there was no doubt but that one Duke Caldwell was in for some unpleasant surprises. Meanwhile, she would keep acting just the same to keep him from suspecting that anything was going to change.

She looked over at the tiny countertop with its compact washbasin and saw that Duke had set out a towel and some soap for her.

"My goodness, just like the Ritz," she murmured to herself. Or was he hinting that her face was dirty? She got up, slipped off her jacket and inspected the arrangement, finding that a spigot on a large container of water was situated just above the basin. There was also a new toothbrush and some toothpaste at hand. She pressed the spigot and nearly jumped out of her skin at the sound of Duke's voice coming from above her head.

"Good morning, Leslie. I trust you slept well. Don't fill the basin too full, or it will splash all over the place if I have to make a sudden stop." When Leslie did not reply, he went on, "I have the intercom on, so I can hear you perfectly well. Go ahead and talk."

"I will when I have something to say," Leslie replied, trying to sound coldly unpleasant but finding it difficult. She felt one hundred percent better this morning, her head clear and her stomach ready for a good breakfast.

"Unusual woman," Duke remarked, sounding quite good-humored himself. "When you've finished cleaning up, look in that box to the right of the door. I put a thermos of coffee and some doughnuts in there for you. If you want some milk and cereal, help yourself."

"Okay, thanks," Leslie replied. She scrubbed her face, brushed her hair and then sat down to pour herself some coffee. "Where are we?" she asked, taking a large bite of a glazed doughnut.

"In Ohio, on Interstate 70. Old Callahan picked me up just after I crossed the border, and he's been staying right behind me ever since. I'll bet he's wondering when I'm going to stop and let you out."

"And I'll bet he isn't." Leslie retorted, feeling her aggravation of the previous day returning. "I don't know any Callahan, and I have no idea where you got all those crazy notions about me. All I know is they're completely wrong."

"Then why is Callahan following me? He's no friend of mine."

"I have no idea," Leslie replied. "Maybe your wife hired him to keep an eye on you. From what I've seen, it wouldn't be a bad idea."

There was a short pause, and then Duke burst out in hearty laughter. "That was as sneaky a way to find out whether I'm married as I've ever heard. The answer is no, I'm not married, and I don't ever plan to be. I'm not the marrying kind."

"That's good news to all of us," Leslie retorted, finishing off a second doughnut with gusto. "Can't I just take a peek to see where we are? This is very strange, sitting here all alone and having your voice coming from over my head.''

"Not a good idea,'' Duke replied. "Callahan could pull alongside at any time and see you.''

Leslie sighed. "I am sick and tired of hearing about this mythical Callahan. How do you happen to know him so well if he's such a shady character? How do I know he even exists?''

"I don't know him well. I've seen him at one terminal or another a few times, and I know that he drives for Phillips's Farms. He's rather distinguished-looking. It doesn't fit at all with his personality so you don't forget him easily. I don't know why Phillips picked him for this assignment. He has other drivers who are more trustworthy.''

"Callahan isn't?''

"I've heard he often deliberately miscounts his load and makes off with the difference. If I wanted to do Phillips a favor, I'd tell him about it. And I am doing you a favor by keeping you away from him.''

"Darn it, Duke, I have nothing to do with the man!'' Leslie cried, feeling suddenly close to tears of sheer frustration, not so much at being Duke's prisoner as at being so completely miscast in the role of some heavy in a drama she did not understand at all.

"I wish I could believe you.'' Duke's voice sounded sincerely regretful. Then it brightened as he said, "At least we're finally on a first-name basis. Maybe soon you'll give me the real story.''

Leslie felt so much like screaming in rage that she had to count to ten before replying. "You have heard it! There is no other story! What I want to know is when you're going to tell me what it is I'm supposed to be doing here. Why would Cliveden Phillips hire me to do whatever it is I'm supposed to be doing?"

There was silence, and then Duke replied, "I'll tell you when we stop for lunch. I want to be able to watch your face when I do."

"Lovely," Leslie growled. "What do I do in the meantime? Sit here in the gloom and twiddle my thumbs?" The compartment seemed even darker than it had the previous day. She glanced toward the little round window, wondering if Duke had covered it. No, he had not. "Why is it so dark today?" she asked. "Is it raining?"

"No, but it looks as if it might anytime. There are tornado watches out for the St. Louis area. Should be over before we get there, though."

"I hope so," Leslie said with a shudder. She had no desire to visit the Land of Oz with Duke Caldwell.

"There are some magazines in that cupboard to the left of the refrigerator," Duke volunteered next, "and I can put on some music if you'd like. Or you could tell me your life's story to pass the time."

"And have you tell me it's all a lie? No, thanks," Leslie said coldly. "I'll read, if I can see well enough. And I don't care for country and western, so you can skip the music as far as I'm concerned."

"And I'd hoped a good night's sleep might improve your disposition," Duke commented dryly. "There's a little high-intensity reading lamp on the wall above the bunk. You can use that to read by if you promise not to try anything like signaling out the window with it."

"What makes you think you can trust me, even if I do promise?"

"Because you do believe I'll turn you over to Callahan if you try anything, and I don't think you want that."

Leslie frowned. Did she believe that he would? Yesterday she had been sure of it, but today... She shook her head. *Don't let a few smiles and seductive kisses fool you, Leslie,* she warned herself. He still thought she was some kind of criminal. And Callahan didn't sound like anyone she'd like to meet.

She rinsed off her sticky fingers and then investigated the magazines. There were some business magazines, some general interest and several old copies of *Produce Quarterly.* She took most of them out and tossed them on the bunk.

"If you'd like some different music," Duke's voice sounded, "there are some cassette tapes in my duffel bag on the floor."

"I doubt your taste would appeal to me," Leslie said, reaching for the light.

"Damn it, why don't you look instead of jumping to conclusions!" Duke snapped.

"My, my, aren't we testy," Leslie retorted. "Sleep didn't do much for you, either. All right, I'll look." She leaned off the bunk and opened the duffel bag, feeling for the small plastic cassette cases and pulling out several. He eyes widened as she found that they were all classics, many of them her own favorites.

"I admit you surprise me," she said. "I like them all. How do I get them to you?"

"Just open the zipper a little and slide them under. I can reach them."

Leslie did so, commenting, "I feel like a prisoner trying to get a message to the outside world."

"The prison's of your own making," Duke said gruffly.

Leslie shrugged and returned to the magazines. It shouldn't be for much longer, she thought.

Several Beethoven concertos later Duke announced, "I'm going to turn into a big truck stop ahead. I'll fuel up and then pull into their lot for a lunch break. Just stay put until I join you."

"What else would I do?" Leslie asked bitterly. She had kept one ear alert for a police siren, but there had been none. Surely there should have been an all-points bulletin out for Duke's truck by now. It had also occurred to her that, if the man called Callahan really was following them, he might be after her, not Duke. He might have seen her get into the truck and assumed that she was some kind of traveling prostitute. That thought and the memory of his vulgar-sounding voice made her skin crawl. She hated to think what an encounter with the man might be like. Duke Caldwell was definitely preferable.

She had also learned quite a lot from the several old *Produce Quarterly* issues she had thumbed through. Duke was indeed listed on the masthead as one of the West Coast editors, but that fact had escaped her notice before. All of her dealings had been with the East Coast editorial staff, and none of the issues she had studied had had articles on Buena Suerte Farms or their famous owner. From the back issues Duke had, she had gleaned some information that she thought might explain the conflict between Duke and Cliveden Phillips, a subject on which she intended to question Duke very shortly.

There was quite a lot of starting and stopping and maneuvering at the truck stop during which time Leslie thought she again heard the voice of one Mr. Callahan, a fact which Duke confirmed when he came through the doorway to the accompaniment of suddenly very loud country music.

"Thought that might mask the sound of our conversation better," he said with an apologetic grin and wink. "Callahan's parked right next to us. He asked about you again." He sat down close beside Leslie where she sat propped against the pillows. "Enjoy your morning?" he asked softly.

"Not much," Leslie replied, pushing her hair back from her face and turning to look at him. She felt a strange, quivering sensation in her chest as she did so. How could a man who looked so strong and honest and handsome be so—so determined to mistrust her? An ache merged with the quivering inside her, and she looked down. "Why don't you just call the police to come and get me and be done with it?" she asked.

Duke turned Leslie's face back toward his with one large hand, his thumb stroking her cheek as he answered. "For several reasons. Number one, I simply want to prevent Cliveden Phillips from executing his plan and teach him that I'm not someone to try this kind of nonsense on. I don't want to make a public spectacle of him. He has enough personal troubles of his own right now. And I don't want to see you in any trouble with the law, either. I think this is probably your first real mistake, and I doubt you're headed for a life of crime. So it's better all around if I just keep you with me until you give me the information I want."

"But there isn't any to give! Why won't you believe me? I've never had anyone call me a liar before. Never in my whole life!"

"Mainly because Callahan's still out there," Duke replied with a grimace. "There's no other reason he'd be sticking to me like glue."

Leslie sighed. She felt so torn between two conflicting desires that her head felt dizzy. On the one hand, Duke's gentle touch was mesmerizing, his velvet-soft voice hard to connect with words that made her so angry and confused that she wished she was big enough to grab him and beat him into believing her. She shook her head and pushed Duke's hand away.

"This is all wrong. I don't know what to tell you anymore. I do know that I'll soon be reported missing, if I haven't been already, and you'll be in real trouble then. Besides that, I have a fashion photographing job in St. Louis on Monday. Can't you get away from that man long enough to drop me off there? I have friends there I can stay with."

Duke recaptured her face and stared intently into her eyes.

"If you can explain why Callahan is following me, unless it's to put me in a very compromising position, I'll be glad to let you go." He smiled roguishly. "Well, maybe not glad, but I'd let you. Otherwise, I'm going to keep you with me as far as California if necessary, at which time I'll get you and Phillips and Callahan together. Then we'll get some answers."

"But I can't stay that long!" Leslie cried. "I have a job to do in St. Louis. My reputation as a photographer will be ruined if I don't show up!"

"Shhh. My reputation as a person will be ruined if I let you go and your story about life in a traveling bordello makes the news. I'm afraid I have to consider that more important."

"What story? I'm a photographer, not a writer, and you've got my cameras. Besides, such a story wouldn't be true, and you could sue for libel."

"I'm sure there are a lot of reporters who would be delighted to write such a spicy story for you, with all the details about the trip you could supply. Even if a libel suit did succeed, the damage would have been done."

Leslie glared impotently at the darkly handsome face so close to hers. "I hate you. I hate everything about you, but especially your arrogance and your stupidity. It probably won't even sink into that thick skull of yours when you do find out how wrong you've been."

She continued to glare as Duke's eyes wandered over her face, narrowed thoughtfully, glinting with a challenging fire as they met her eyes, and then traveled back down to her lips. It took a strong act of will to keep her tongue from flicking out to moisten those lips, now swollen and nervously dry. *He's going to kiss me,* she thought, even before his hand went around behind her neck. She tried to stiffen and pull away, but he leaned against her, burying them both against the pillows as his mouth found hers and opened to cover it.

Leslie was determined not to respond this time. She valiantly kept her eyes open and her mouth shut, watching the blur of Duke's lushly thick, black curling lashes fan out against his cheeks as he closed his eyes. His tongue repeated its tricks of yesterday, except this time his grasp on her was more gentle, one hand caressing the back of her neck and the other arm enfolding her closely.

"Don't be stubborn, little darling," he murmured. "Your body is already telling me that you want this as much as I do. You're so warm and soft." He nibbled at one corner of her mouth, then traced the edges with his tongue.

"Stop it," Leslie said weakly, trying to turn her head away. She knew her body was doing its best to betray her again. The heat that was generated between them was a chemical reaction that, if confined in a test tube, might well cause an explosion. Why did it have to be this man who set her afire as she had never been before? Why? she wondered as, willy-nilly, her lips softened beneath the onslaught, and her tongue tasted the intruder hungrily. She must resist, for the path she was going down was clearly marked, and though she had never traveled it to the end before, she knew that this man could lead her there with ease if she but let him. She tried pushing against him with her hands, which were caught between them, but he calmly tucked them in tighter and cupped one breast gently, his fingers seeking the peak through her sweater, and finding it.

Was that me? Leslie thought wonderingly as a soft moan escaped her, a response to the wave of sensations that coursed down through her loins at Duke's touch. Were those her hands that were now behind Duke's head, pulling him close instead of pushing him away, stealing into the thick, cool silkiness of his black, black hair? Where was her will to fight? She never let men touch her like that! She opened her eyes, preparing to protest, but the words disappeared from her mind as she gazed into eyes that seemed to burn into her very soul. All she could do was lie breathlessly still as Duke pushed her sweater up and unfastened her bra with a practiced deftness.

"What a beautifully womanly woman," he said huskily, his eyes gazing raptly at her full breasts, their peaks swollen and eager for his touch. He lowered lips sensuous and warm to one and covered the other with a caressing hand.

Another gasping moan came from Leslie's lips as floods of desire threatened their banks. She felt Duke fumbling with the button at the waistband of her slacks and drew in a rasping breath, a great aching emptiness following the rough caress of his fingers on the soft skin of her belly. She could not stop him now. She did not want to stop him.

Suddenly Duke uttered a muffled curse, jerked his head up and withdrew his hand, then roughly pulled her sweater down.

"Damn it!" he swore, raking his black hair back from his forehead with a tense, angry gesture as he sat back and glared darkly at Leslie. "Why do you, of all women, have to make me lose control like that?"

"My sentiments exactly," Leslie snapped in return, scrambling into a sitting position, hating herself for the burning frustration she felt. Her fingers trembled as she refastened her bra.

"Don't make me laugh," Duke rasped, shaking his head and still glowering. "You were having a wonderful time, and most willingly. You seemed determined to do old Phillips's bidding, even though it will get you nowhere."

"I didn't notice anyone pushing you!" Leslie shot back, smoothing her hair back from her damp forehead. "And I was not doing it for anyone. It was some kind of base...animal instinct that I hate even more than you do. Just stay away from me from now on."

"Gladly." Duke frowned a moment longer, then dropped his head forward, rubbing his neck tiredly. "God, that leaves me feeling rotten. I suppose I'd better have some lunch, though. I can't stay parked here all day."

"Let me fix something. I feel like pacing around in my cage," Leslie suggested, jumping to her feet, glad for anything to divert her attention from the mesmerizing face of Duke Caldwell. And, she told herself, it would be a good idea to keep his mind on other things as well! She began rummaging in the cupboards for various items she had noticed on an earlier inspection, and at the same time continued talking. "I thought you were going to tell me what my role in this wild story of yours is supposed to be," she said as she set out paper plates and began constructing some sandwiches with luncheon meats and cheeses. She glanced back at Duke, who was now lounging on the bunk, watching her thoughtfully. When he did not reply, she went on. "Does it have something to do with the water rights issue that you and Phillips are at odds over? I read about it in one of those old *Produce Quarterly*s."

Duke nodded then and returned to sitting upright on the edge of the bunk, his chin on his hand.

"It's still a very live issue. Phillips has a long-standing claim on far more of the water in the Imperial Valley than he has any right to have, especially with the salinization problems we're having now as the result of years of irrigation. Thousands of acres are going out of production every year without the necessary water to use new techniques to flush the salt away. He's deathly afraid that, if I get into Congress, I'll eventually get enough clout to break his hold. He knows I'm a sure bet to beat one of his political hack cronies in the election next fall unless he can destroy my reputation as a knight in shining armor with the constituents in the district."

Leslie paused in spreading the mustard on one sandwich and shook her head in disbelief.

"You mean that just finding you'd been making a little whoopee in your truck could get you defeated, even though you're not married? I find that hard to believe in this day and age. Or were you lying about not being married?"

"No, I wasn't lying. It's a very conservative, religious constituency, and while I doubt there are many who think I lead a celibate life, they do appreciate discretion. Their families are important, as is the image of anyone who would be an example for their children. Blatantly immoral behavior, or what they perceive as such, would make my chances less than slim."

"And you think I'm here to seduce you and somehow get a compromising picture or two?" Leslie asked incredulously as she handed Duke a plate with two monumental sandwiches on it. "Have you any idea how difficult that would be in here? I'm a photographer, not a magician. And there's one other thing that you haven't taken into account."

"What's that?" Duke asked, taking a huge bite of his sandwich and nodding in approval. "Good," he said.

"The fact that I'd rather be dead than be in a picture like that myself," Leslie replied.

Duke looked up and stared at her intently, and Leslie stared back unflinchingly. *For goodness' sake, man, you must be able to see that that's the truth!* she thought.

"Explain Callahan," he said, dropping his eyes.

"I can't!" Leslie cried, frustrated once more. "Which reminds me, there's something you said that doesn't make much sense. Why, if you think Phillips is out to practically wreck your life, are you so sensitive about whatever personal problems he's having?''

Duke looked up, one eyebrow raised and a wry little smile on his face as he replied, ''Just because he's a bastard doesn't mean I have to be one, does it?''

He chuckled as Leslie shot back disgustedly, ''I don't think the question is open.''

''I knew you were the wrong person to ask,'' Duke said with an easy, adorable grin that had Leslie feeling uncomfortably warm and friendly again when she wanted to feel nothing but cold and angry.

She tilted her chin upward and asked frostily, ''Just how does it happen that you are so familiar with Mr. Phillips's problems?''

''How does it happen that you're not?'' Duke countered. ''It was in all of the newspapers about a year ago last January.''

''I was in Lebanon then,'' Leslie replied, feeling a bit smug as Duke's face quickly lost its superior expression. ''Maybe you should fill me in.''

''It's not a minor problem,'' Duke said, fixing Leslie with a serious look. ''Phillips, whatever his faults, has always been extremely devoted to his children by his late first wife, and to his grandchildren. A year ago last January his seven-year-old grandson was apparently kidnapped. Unfortunately, I guess, it was not done by someone who wanted a large ransom but by one of those people who just wanted a child. Phillips offered a huge reward, but no trace of the boy has ever been found.''

''Oh, no!'' Leslie cried sympathetically. ''How dreadful.''

Duke nodded. ''It certainly is. That part, of course, is public knowledge. I also happen to know that Phillips's daughter, the boy's mother, has not been able to cope with it, and she is now in a psychiatric hospital.''

"What a tragedy." Leslie shook her head. "I don't understand how anyone can do that to a child or his family." She studied Duke's somber expression. He really was concerned for the other man, in spite of everything. "I can certainly see why you feel the way you do," she said softly.

Duke broke the sober mood with a little nod of affirmation and a sudden smile. "Now I have a question for you," he said.

"Fire away," Leslie said with a sigh, expecting more questions about how and when she had contacted the infamous Cliveden Phillips.

Instead, Duke asked, "How does such an attractive young lady as Miss Leslie Lyon happen to have stayed single for—what is it?—twenty-five years? It seems unlikely you haven't had any offers of marital bliss."

Leslie looked away from those dark eyes that were beginning to disturb her inner workings again.

"I'm twenty-seven," she replied, "and, yes, I've had offers. Why is it men always think every woman is just waiting for one of them to cast their line? All through my school years I dreamed of seeing places in the world I'd only read about. When I discovered I had talent for photography, I found that it also gave me the chance I'd been looking for to travel. My chief work is photographing the human side of newsworthy events, anything from wars to royal weddings. I've been to most of the European countries, to the Middle East and the South Pacific. I have a job coming up in El Salvador. I've won several prizes, too. So, you see, settling down to domestic bliss is something that I haven't really considered yet. Maybe someday, if someone comes along who really makes bells rings, I will. Maybe.'' She flicked a quick glance up at Duke through her lashes and for a moment thought she saw a look of respect. He quickly masked it with a cynical lift of his brows as he thoughtfully finished his sandwich.

"So,'' he said finally, "you're a thoroughly modern woman, having a wonderful fling worldwide but planning someday to marry if you run across some fellow who rings your bells without interfering too much with your career.'' He cocked an eyebrow at Leslie. "Lots of luck.''

Leslie was about to issue a hot rebuttal to Duke's statement, but something in the strained, harsh look about his eyes stayed her. There was a clue to his character there, she decided. For all his practiced charm, both his words and his expression, added to everything that had gone before, betrayed a deep mistrust of women in general. So instead of snarling her reply, she merely sighed and said patiently, "Wrong again. I don't have to travel to be a photographer. It's a perfect career to combine with a happy home.''

Duke responded with a short, dry laugh. "If you think you'll ever be content to stay home after all the travel and variety you've enjoyed, you're in for an unpleasant awakening. I hope you realize that before you make a sad mistake.'' Before Leslie could reply, he stood up. "It's time we got moving again before Callahan gets so suspicious he tries to get in here with us.''

Just as Duke began to open the doorway, Leslie heard the sound of a siren in the distance, rapidly growing louder. For a moment her heart almost stopped, then it lurched and began to race, and she struggled to her feet, feeling sick and dizzy.

"Wh-what's that!" she cried, clutching Duke's arm and pointing in the direction of the sound.

Duke cocked his head, then looked down at Leslie's ashen face, his own now gentle and concerned.

"It's just an emergency vehicle up on the highway," he said softly, laying one hand along her cheek reassuringly. "There's probably been an accident. Why are you so frightened?" As Leslie stared at him dumbly, tears coming to her eyes, he shook his head and said soberly, "Did you think I might have called the police? I wouldn't do that, Leslie. Not under any circumstances. We'll thrash this out between us, somehow. Okay?"

Leslie nodded.

"Smile?" Duke suggested, looking at her encouragingly.

Leslie managed a tight little smile, but her lips were trembling as she watched Duke slip through the opening into the driver's compartment. It was only when she felt the truck begin to move that she turned and flung herself on the bunk and buried her face in the pillows, sobbing silently.

What was wrong with her? She had reacted with sheer, heart-stopping panic at the sound of that siren. But she couldn't have been afraid that they were coming for her. She had done nothing wrong. Nor did she think Duke had called them. No, she had not been afraid the police were coming for her; she had been afraid they were coming for Duke! Didn't she want them to come?

CHAPTER FOUR

"GOOD LORD, are you mixed up," Leslie muttered, finally pushing herself to a sitting position and reaching for a nearby box of tissues. She blew her nose so hard that Duke immediately came on the intercom.

"You keeping a goose back there? I thought I heard one honking."

"Hah, hah," Leslie replied thickly. "By doze is ruddig again."

"Those spring colds are hard to shake," Duke said sympathetically. "I've got some milder antihistamines in my duffel bag if you want to try one that won't knock you out."

"Thank you."

But Leslie did not move, merely sat and stared in front of her, trying to analyze her bizarre response to the siren. Was it that Stockholm syndrome that she had read about? She wasn't sure she'd been a captive long enough, and besides, she did not feel that her life was being threatened. Her reaction was, she decided, totally unreasonable, the product of that same flaw in her character, that same overzealous protective reaction that made her ready and willing to pay the repair bill on Ted and Melody's car. Melody had made a mistake that she really ought to pay for, but it would be traumatic for her to have to do so.

Duke had made a mistake that he ought to pay for, too, but should he go to jail? He seemed like a basically nice person, and apparently he had good reason for suspecting that Cliveden Phillips might pull some dirty trick on him. But was that sufficient reason for her to be willing to forget both that he had her penned in this sleeper like a hamster in a cage and that he still believed she was a hired temptress? No, it was not! She had better get her head on a little straighter! Never mind that physically he turned her on like a neon sign. That was absolutely, totally beside the point. Duke Caldwell had abducted her! He deserved to face the consequences. Next time she heard a siren, she would remember that.

With the decision made, Leslie plumped up the pillows on the bunk and sat back, once again thumbing through the old *Produce Quarterly*s. Perhaps she would unearth some clue as to why Duke was considered such a paragon when compared with Cliveden Phillips, even though Phillips, too, was a wealthy landowner. She found what seemed to be the answer in an article that presented statistics on the sizes and corporate structures of the farms in southern California. Buena Suerte was one of the largest farms in total acreage, its value in the millions of dollars. But unlike most of the others, which were either family owned or investor owned, a large part of Buena Suerte was owned by employees who had bought into the corporation on a stock-option plan initiated by Duke Caldwell when he took over the farms upon his father's retirement. Duke still had controlling interest, but the employees took part in management decisions at all levels, and Buena Suerte's profit margin far outshone any of the other farms listed.

No wonder he's up for sainthood, Leslie thought with a wry grimace. Well, things would certainly change when the police caught up with them. And if that didn't blacken his character enough, her lawsuit would finish it off. Loren Barstow would doubtless be delighted to take her case. She could imagine the kind of headlines that Loren's celebrated services would produce: Citrus Magnate Sued For Millions By Woman Photographer After Nightmare Ride Across The Country.

She glanced toward the driving compartment. Except for Callahan, Duke didn't seem quite as convinced as he once had that she was here to seduce him. Maybe he hadn't considered what the consequences might be if he was wrong about her. It wouldn't hurt to try to use that argument to persuade him to let her off in St. Louis. If he did, she wouldn't press charges against him. *I'll try that approach next time we stop,* she decided with a nod of satisfaction.

With that second decision made, Leslie picked up a more readable magazine and was soon engrossed in a sizzling story about a female spy who seduced her way into the bedrooms of assorted powerful men, a story that faded into a dream as she dozed off. In her dream she became a scantily clad seductress, making off with an envelope of secret documents, until a shot rang out.

"My God, what was that!" Leslie cried, her heart racing as she suddenly came awake enough to separate dream from reality. The shot had seemed so terribly real!

"Thunder," Duke replied over the intercom. "Lightning hit close by. Were you asleep?"

"I guess I dozed off," Leslie answered, still feeling shaky. "I dreamed I'd been shot."

"Guilty conscience?" Duke suggested dryly.

"Hardly," Leslie snapped back, fully awake now. So he was still at it. Well, she'd give him some food for thought very soon. Through the tiny window it looked almost as dark as night. "Where are we?" she asked. "Almost to St. Louis?"

"No, we're still almost a hundred miles east of there. I've had to slow down in this storm. I'm going to look for the first place to stop. There are tornado warnings out until eleven o'clock tonight, along with hailstorms and high winds. No point in driving into that."

Leslie groaned and chewed her lip pensively. She had hoped that Duke would make it to St. Louis tonight. That was apparently a lost cause. Why hadn't the police found them? Surely it wouldn't be that hard to track his truck. Well, they hadn't. But Susan would have noticed by now that she was absent, and she might well report her missing. *God, I hope she doesn't call my parents or Melody,* Leslie thought with a wave of anxiety. They would be so terribly frightened!

"Duke?" she said quickly.

"What?"

"You've either got to let me out or do something for me when we stop."

"What's that?"

"My neighbor, Susan Martin, will have noticed by now that I'm missing. If she calls my parents or my sister, they'll be terrified. I have to get word to her that I'm all right."

There was silence for several minutes, and then Duke said, "All right, I'll send a telegram for you. Write down what you want to tell her, but don't try any coded messages. I'm not stupid enough to fall for that."

He was incredibly stupid, Leslie thought, glaring in his direction, but all she said was "Thanks." For some reason he didn't seem nearly as friendly as he had earlier. He must have spent the past few hours convincing himself that he'd been right about her all along. That might ruin her chances of talking him into letting her go in St. Louis, but she had to try, anyway.

It was not long before they pulled into a huge truck stop, and Leslie could tell by the sound of throbbing diesel engines that many other truckers had decided to sit out the storm and were keeping their engines running, ready to go when the storm let up.

Duke made his way into the sleeper and turned on the light, and Leslie's heart sank at the decidedly cold and stiff set to his features. He had definitely reverted to the antagonist.

"Got your message ready?" he asked briefly.

Leslie nodded silently and handed it to him. She had written, "On my way to St. Louis. Tell Molly I'll see her there Monday bright and early, and call Melody to tell her I'll call her from there."

Duke read the message and frowned. "I can't send this. You may not be there. Who or what is Molly? A code for something? And why make a point of calling Melody?"

"I will too be there," Leslie snarled, jumping to her feet and glaring at him. "I have to be there. Melody is my sister. I talk to her almost every day when I'm in New York, and if she calls for ages and there's no answer, she'll be worried. And, no, Molly is not a code, she's a model! Molly Primrose. You'd recognize her in a minute, since she's been on more magazine covers than any other woman in history."

"Oh, *that* Molly," Duke said with an expressive lift of his brows. "We've met."

I'll bet you have, Leslie thought grimly. They would make a fine pair, a couple of self-centered, suspicious egomaniacs. Aloud she said, "There are a couple of things I'd like you to think about before you give me any more nonsense about keeping me in this stinking hole for another three days." She paused for a breath, and Duke arched a skeptical eyebrow at her.

"What things?" he asked, one corner of his mouth curving upward in a rather nasty little smile.

Leslie took a deep breath, fixed her eyes on Duke's and then spat out the words as coldly and precisely as she could. "Number one, you are wrong about me and, as a result, you will eventually find yourself in trouble with the law. That should do your precious reputation plenty of damage. Not only that, but in addition to whatever criminal charges are appropriate, I intend to sue you for every penny you've got. With the legal counsel I've got, I should have no trouble winning. What chance will you have of being elected to Congress then, I wonder?"

To Leslie's distress, Duke's expression did not change at all. In fact, he shrugged.

"I've thought of all that," he said as if it were a matter of extreme indifference, "but I think I'll still go with my original hunch as long as Mr. Callahan stays as close as a Siamese twin. I am curious, though, about what legal counsel you intend to engage to impoverish me."

"Loren Barstow," Leslie replied. "He's an old friend of mine and my parents."

"Really? Mine, too," Duke said, grinning triumphantly as Leslie's face fell. "As a matter of fact, he's the one who talked me into going into politics. We'll have to see who gets to him first, won't we?"

He chuckled as Leslie muttered, "You worm!"

"Now about this message. Why should this supposed neighbor be involved in your business affairs?"

Leslie tried to keep cool as she explained, but she felt a helpless rage beginning to mount again at the coldly indifferent look on Duke's face.

It exploded after he said, "Well, I'll think of something to tell her. Maybe I'll just call her up and tell her we're eloping, and you've decided to retire from photography to raise a family."

"For God's sake, be reasonable!" she cried hoarsely. "You can't do that. She'd call my parents immediately to see if they'd heard about it. She'd suspect right away something was wrong if she didn't hear it from me. Please, just send that message."

Duke twisted his mouth thoughtfully. "All right," he said finally. "Maybe we'll get this all straightened out in time, although I doubt it."

"Thank goodness!" Leslie said fervently. She hated the image she had of her parents waiting anxiously by the telephone for some word of their missing daughter. They had barely recovered from the scare they'd had when she had been mistakenly reported missing in Beirut last year.

"I'm afraid I'm going to have to leave you in the dark while I go into the restaurant to eat," Duke said next.

Leslie glared at him helplessly. Was there no end to the unpleasantness of this man? "Why?"

"So Callahan can't peek in and see you," he replied. "He's got a ladder in his truck. I'll try to keep an eye on him, but I'm damned if I'll eat with him. If you hear anything, just keep very quiet, and for God's sake, don't open the door for him." As Leslie continued to scowl sullenly, he suddenly looked more worried than hostile. "Promise me!" he said firmly, lifting her chin with his hand. "Promise me, Leslie."

"Of course I won't let him in," Leslie said, jerking her chin away angrily. "I don't know the man, and I don't want to know him. For that matter, I don't want to know you, either. What am I supposed to do, stay here and eat baloney sandwiches forever, wearing these same clothes for days and days? I'm going to smell like a goat pretty soon." She looked away as Duke's face underwent a transformation, a little quirk at the corner of his mouth growing into an adorably warm and friendly smile. What had she done to cause that? Or was it simply a change he made to suit the situation? He was the strangest man!

"I'm afraid they don't sell ladies' wear at a truck stop," he said, "but they may have some sweatshirts or T-shirts. I'll see. I can pretend I'm buying some for my housekeeper's kids. And I'll smuggle you out a hot dog, somehow. Okay?"

"I guess it will have to be," Leslie replied tightly, determined not to fall under the spell of Duke's alter ego this time. How adept he was at turning into Mr. Likable just when she was ready to tear him limb from limb. It was probably designed to keep her off balance, but it wouldn't work much longer. She was catching on.

"I'll be as quick as possible," Duke said, turning off the light and plunging the sleeper into near darkness.

"Don't hurry on my account," Leslie said coldly. She heard the sound of the zipper opening then closing, but was aware that Duke had not left. The light came back on.

"Forgot my rain poncho," he said, grinning and taking the cloak from a hook. He slipped it on. "Now

I'm ready." He paused to wink at Leslie. "You're a very distracting woman, Leslie Lyon."

"Stuff it," she replied, feeling quite pleased with herself that she hadn't given him the satisfaction of responding to his smile and wink. "Oooh!" she gasped, as suddenly there was a large hand on either side of her face, and warm lips unerringly found hers in a short but breathtaking kiss.

"I had to be sure you'd miss me," Duke whispered. Then he whirled in a rustle of nylon and plastic and left Leslie feeling too confused to whip off a quick retort.

"Darn him anyway!" Leslie muttered when the truck door slammed behind him. She rubbed the rough sleeve of her sweater across her lips to try to erase the tingling warmth his lips had left behind, like a brand. His continual switching from antagonist to seducer was far more difficult to cope with than if he simply stayed coldly hostile. Still, it was preferable to his being constantly seductive. The mutual physical attraction between them would be impossible for her to fight off alone. Putty in his hands might be an apt description of the way she would be then, she thought wryly. As it was, she felt as nervous and on edge as she had when she'd been caught between warring factions in Beirut. And sitting alone in the dark, while intermittent flashes of lightning from the diminishing storm illuminated the sleeper, did nothing to calm her nerves. It was like a ghostly light show with sound effects, occasional loud claps of thunder that sent shivers down her spine. It set off far too graphic memories of the real terror she had felt when bombs were falling near the building where she had taken shelter.

I'd better get my mind on something else, Leslie thought, noticing that her hands were icy and trem-

bling. Surely no one outside would notice the tiny
reading light if she kept it focused on a book. She found
the switch and attempted to read an article on rose cul-
tivation, a topic close to her mother's heart but not one
which fascinated Leslie.

Suddenly, in the midst of the sound of thunder and
wind, she heard the scratch of something metallic
against the side of the sleeper. Quickly she switched off
her light and listened intently. What could it be? Could
it be Callahan putting up his ladder against the truck to
peek into the window of the sleeper? She had no sooner
finished the thought than a beam of light penetrated the
darkness, sweeping across the far wall. With one quick
move Leslie rolled off the bunk and onto the floor, lying
as far beneath the edge of the bunk as she could, in an
area she was sure would not be visible no matter how
anyone contorted himself to peer inside.

God, I wish Duke would come back, she thought, her
heart pounding. Whatever Duke Caldwell's faults, he
was far preferable to this weird Callahan person, whose
reason for following them was certainly bizarre, maybe
even sadistic. If he did think she was a prostitute...
There had been several cases in recent years of psy-
chotic killers, whose deranged minds led them to serial
killings of young women. She lay still, afraid to move,
even when she thought she heard the ladder being removed. Then, after what seemed like hours, there was
a scraping sound and a blast of cold air as the door
opened. Was Duke finally back, or was it...?

When first the radio came on followed by the light in
the sleeper, her rush of relief told Leslie just how
frightened she had been.

"What are you doing down there?" Duke inquired,
his eyebrows arching together in puzzlement at the sight

of Leslie emerging from her hiding place. As Leslie explained, his quizzical frown turned into a dark scowl. "Damn it! If I hadn't been so busy running errands of mercy for you, I might have caught him. But then—" his mouth twisted into a wry smile "—if it weren't for you, he wouldn't have been there, would he?" He glanced toward the window. "We'd better cover that up tonight."

"I wish this storm would stop," Leslie said, starting at another clap of thunder.

For the first time Duke seemed to notice Leslie's still-ashen face. He set a large grocery bag down on the little countertop, flung his poncho over the hook and then sat down beside her. He placed a large shiny bag on her lap.

"Forget about old Callahan and the storm," he said, enfolding her with a comforting arm and moving closer. "We're safe and warm in here. See if those will relieve the clothing problem." He smiled as beguilingly as a fond uncle bringing a surprise gift to a favorite niece.

Leslie eyed him suspiciously, more unsettled than ever by the warmth of his closeness. Now what was he up to?

"Did you send the telegram?" she asked.

"Of course. I said I would, didn't I?" Duke looked insulted at the suggestion that he might not have done so, and Leslie looked away from his accusing eyes. What right did he have to be so short-tempered about having his honesty questioned, when he did the same to her all the time? She started to snap out a reply along those lines and then thought better of it. What was the use?

"Come on, look inside," Duke said impatiently so, with a sigh, Leslie opened the bag and pulled out the contents.

"My goodness," she said, her eyes widening as she held up first one soft sweatshirt and then another, each with matching sweatpants. One set was black, a parade of white ducks marching across the shirt, the other pink and sporting a row of fuzzy white rabbits. She looked up at Duke. "These are...very nice. Thank you. It will help a lot. But I'm not sure I need two sets."

"You may," Duke replied cryptically. He reached into the bag and drew out a pair of moccasins with fleece linings. "Here. Hope they fit. At least now you can put these things on and wash your underwear if you want to." He grinned mischievously. "They had more stuff than I expected in there, but no ladies' lingerie."

"I expect you'd be an expert on that," Leslie commented dryly.

Duke chuckled. "Not really. I've never bought any, if you must know the truth. In fact, I've always stuck to jewelry and perfume where ladies are concerned. It's safer. Now why don't you put on one of those outfits, and we'll have some hot dogs with all the trimmings. Callahan wasn't in the diner, for obvious reasons, so I brought everything back here, and it's getting cold."

Leslie picked up the pink suit, then fixed Duke with a severe look.

"I'm not changing with you in here," she said stiffly. "Would you please go up in front for a minute?" She felt Duke's arm tighten about her and saw the devilish glint come into his eyes. Here comes that old line about the human body being nothing to be ashamed of, she thought resignedly, preparing for an argument.

Instead, to her surprise, Duke nuzzled her cheek briefly and then replied, "Of course, but hurry. I'm starved."

Why am I so nervous? Leslie wondered as her fingers fumbled with the simple chore of getting the tags and labels off her new clothes. Thunder and lightning had always unsettled her, more so since her experiences in Lebanon, but it was not only that. It seemed that each new encounter with Duke Caldwell was more unnerving than the last. Why? He had done nothing this time, except kindly furnish her with something to put on besides the sweater and slacks she had worn for two days and politely leave so that she could change. She was fairly sure now that he meant her no physical harm, but emotionally...

Well, who wouldn't be a wreck, being held prisoner like this? she consoled herself as she slipped into the fleecy, soft suit and thrust her feet into the slippers, which fit perfectly.

"Ready," she called as she folded her other clothing and tucked it under the bunk.

"Be there in a minute," Duke answered. "I'm watching Callahan. He's doing something peculiar."

"What was he doing?" Leslie asked when Duke appeared a few minutes later.

"I don't know. He lifted a large bag out of his trunk. It seemed to be quite heavy the way he struggled with it. I can't imagine he'd be doing laundry now, but he carried it into the building where they have some coin washing machines."

"Maybe he's smuggling something," Leslie suggested.

"Not likely," Duke said with a chuckle as he began to unload their dinner from the bag. "It would have to be gold, as heavy as it seemed to be, and I doubt he's into anything like that." His eyes swept over Leslie appreciatively. "Pink becomes you," he said, giving her a smile that lighted every corner of the small room. "You do a lot for that warm-up suit, too."

"Thanks," Leslie replied tightly, feeling a ridiculous flush rise to her cheeks. She did not want Duke to look at her like that. It made her feel more vulnerable than ever. She would feel far safer if he were still angry with her. Perhaps she could find some topic, besides that annoying one about her supposed mission for Cliveden Phillips, that would put him off.

"Is your hot dog all right?" Duke asked. "I had them put everything on it."

"Fine. Delicious," Leslie replied. She was suddenly aware that she had eaten half of it and barely noticed the taste. Duke had placed a large package of potato chips and two chocolate milk shakes on a tray between them on the edge of the bunk. Leslie took a few swallows of her milk shake, which was so rich and thick that she could hardly get it through the straw. She cast about her mind for something to discuss, but nothing useful suggested itself.

Duke was quiet, too, apparently absorbed in eating. He startled Leslie by asking, "How long have you been a photographer?"

"I—I guess you could say since college," she answered. "I took a course in it just to fill in some hours I needed and fell in love with it. After that, photography was all I wanted to do. Why?"

"Just curious. I wondered how a person got into the profession."

"I worked for a newspaper for a while," Leslie added, "and started free-lancing on the side. It took a while before I could make enough to live on without a regular job. Have you always run a farm?"

Duke shook his head. "I went to law school, intending to practice law, but my father...had a bitter divorce and started drinking heavily. The farms started going downhill. I couldn't see letting that happen, after all the years he'd worked to build them up, so I convinced him to turn the reins over to me. That was ten years ago." He gave Leslie a quirky smile. "I'm thirty-five, in case you wondered."

"Mmmm," Leslie replied noncommittally, although she had been curious. Duke was one of those men who would look very much the same until he was past fifty. A bitter divorce. Perhaps that was why he was determined not to marry. "Is your father better now?" she asked tactfully.

"Not really," Duke answered, his face suddenly grim. "His drinking is under control, but he'll never recover emotionally, I'm afraid. He adored my mother, although he probably did spend more time at his work than was good for their marriage. He had no idea she wasn't content in her role as wife and mother until she left him for a man who offered her a chance to play at being a businesswoman, as well, with her own little corporation to run. That would have been bad enough, but the man she left home for was someone my father hated. Cliveden Phillips."

"Clive—" Leslie almost choked. Duke's mother was Mrs. Cliveden Phillips, the wife of the man who produced Fling! The woman who had wanted a man who looked like Duke to be the Fling man!

"What's the matter?" Duke demanded. "Have you met her? Was she the one who hired you?"

"No!" Leslie almost shouted. "No one hired me! Will you please get that through your thick head? It's just that someone at the advertising agency mentioned that she had... some interest in the Fling promotion." Something told her not to mention what that interest was, a premonition she was soon glad for.

"Really?" He arched one eyebrow, his eyes narrowed and coldly glittering. "Maybe she's getting interested in younger men. Old Clive had better watch out."

Obviously, Leslie thought, Duke and his mother did not get along well. In fact, if he thought she might have hired Leslie to destroy her own son's political ambitions, he must think that she hated him as much as he seemed to despise her. How very sad. Especially since the woman's choice for the type of man she hoped to see in the Fling advertisements indicated she admired her son very much. *I wonder what Duke would think if he knew?* Leslie pondered, sure from what he had said that he had no idea of his mother's interest. It was not something she could ask him directly. Instead, she asked, "Do you see your mother often?" and immediately felt as if she had blundered into a hornet's nest.

"Never," Duke replied, "and I never plan to. She was only too glad to be rid of me, as well, since I took my father's side against her. At first she used to try to get in touch with me from time to time, but she's given up in recent years. I guess she finally understood that I wanted nothing more to do with her."

"Duke, that's terrible," Leslie said reprovingly. "I'm sure your mother misses you. You should go to see her."

"I don't need your advice, thanks," Duke said, giving her an icy look, "especially when you don't know what you're talking about. She chose a new, exciting life over her husband and son. Let her live with her decision."

Leslie frowned. "I can't imagine that you really believe that she stopped loving you. Or are you one of those men who doesn't believe it's possible for a woman to combine a career and marriage? That somehow having a career keeps her from having normal emotions?"

"I've never seen the combination work well. As for having normal emotions, who knows what those are anymore? Most women are just like my mother, thinking they want one thing and then finding out later they want something else, and putting whatever it is they want ahead of anything else."

"Oh, for heaven's sake, Duke," Leslie snapped, "that's ridiculous. Women still love their husbands and children as much as they ever did. They've just found out that you don't have to stay home all the time in order to be a good wife and mother, and there are plenty of men who don't mind if their wives have another interest and earn an extra paycheck. But I certainly understand now why you're determined to keep on your blinders, swim against the tide and never marry. It's really too bad that you've made so many poor decisions based on something that you may not have understood completely in the first place and show no signs of understanding now."

Duke flung his napkin down and glared at Leslie. "What in hell are you talking about? You say you don't even know my mother."

"I don't," Leslie replied calmly, "but I doubt you ever did, either. Did you ever try to find out her side of the story? I'll bet there was a lot more to it than a little neglect and some greener pastures."

"Let's drop the subject," Duke growled, standing and turning away as he began to dispose of the trash from their dinner. "Your response is just what I'd predict from someone who expects bells to ring when she meets Mr. Right, and then to get married and live happily ever after, just like in some fairy tale. I'm glad I won't be around to tell you I told you so when it all falls apart.''

"Poor Duke," Leslie said sarcastically, "so afraid he might make a mistake that he's willing to put up with a lifetime of shallow relationships with shallow women. Well, have fun while you can. Someday you'll be old and lonely and wonder why you didn't risk it.''

"I doubt that," Duke snapped, whirling back around to glare at Leslie. "I've had a great many very meaningful relationships with women. I suppose some of them might even have been called 'love' by a romantic like you. But that doesn't require marriage. And, thank God, neither does sex nowadays. So why tie a knot that will cause nothing but pain if it comes undone after the love fades away, as it usually does? It's stupid.''

Leslie slanted a look up at Duke. She had certainly struck a nerve. Might as well drive home the needle a little more. At least this conversation had kept him from turning on his more seductive talents.

"I'm sorry," she said, "but I don't think it's stupid at all. I happen to believe in love and marriage that last, and in sex within the bonds of matrimony. I guess I'm not the modern woman you thought me after all. I'm certainly not like the ones you're used to.''

Duke sat back down with a thud and leaned toward Leslie, staring at her incredulously. "You can't be serious," he said.

"Why can't I?"

He shook his head and laughed. "Do you expect me to believe that a woman with your career, your passionate nature, someone who travels all over as you do, has never—"

"Oh, for heaven's sake!" Leslie interrupted. "You sound like the same old broken record as the rest! Where is it written that all virgins are supposed to be prim little ingenues? Why is it my career is supposed to make it necessary for me to have had worldwide sexual experience, too? I haven't. You can believe it or not, as you see fit, but I'm sure you won't, considering your preconceptions about what all women are like and the fact that you think I'm lying most of the time." She jerked her head away as Duke placed his finger beneath her chin.

"I'm sorry," Duke said, taking a firm grip on Leslie's chin and turning her face toward his. "I didn't mean to make fun of you." He studied her face thoughtfully, his own expression becoming gentle. "I think it's just that I don't know quite what to make of you, Leslie Lyon. But I do believe you." He smiled the adorable, deep-dimpled smile that did strange things to Leslie's equilibrium. "Talk about swimming against the tide! I think you're the first virgin I've run into since high school."

"More's the pity," Leslie said tightly, wondering if Duke knew that she was not at all sure how long she would remain in that condition if he were to turn on his charm full power. Suddenly they were both distracted by what sounded like someone pelting the sleeper with rocks.

"What's that?" Leslie cried.

"Hailstones, I'm afraid," Duke replied. "I didn't want to worry you, but they were predicting one more wave of severe storms before this system is past us. I think we might as well just get into bed and pull the covers over our heads. The storm can't get to us, but you might feel better if you can't hear it." He grinned. "I can put Beethoven's Ninth Symphony on the cassette player full blast. That will help mask the sound of the storm."

Leslie felt her throat constrict. Duke was talking about getting into bed as casually as if it were something she was supposed to take as a matter of course. But it wasn't, not to her. And it certainly wasn't that she felt he was likely to attack her. It was...almost the reverse! And in that sleeping bag, as large as it was, there wasn't much extra room.

"Maybe I'll...just get under the sleeping bag again," she stammered hoarsely. "Sleeping bags make me...claustrophobic."

Duke cocked a knowing eyebrow at her as he stood up and started stripping off his shirt.

"Only if you have to share them, I'll bet," he commented, giving her an irrepressible wink. "Tell you what. You can stay on this side and leave the zipper down so that you can escape in a flash if I bother you, which I promise I won't do—even though I'd like to."

"You don't think I'll go for my cameras?"

"No," Duke said slowly, "I don't think you will."

"Well, all right," Leslie said, privately wondering if Duke was really beginning to believe in her innocence or if he just thought she wasn't capable of jimmying the padlock.

"Good," Duke said, flashing his dimpled smile. "I expected you to put up more of an argument than that. Maybe you're beginning to believe I'm not such an ogre after all. Time to turn your back, Miss Lyon."

Darn, Leslie thought as she did as commanded and felt her upper lip bead with perspiration at the sound of

Duke's clothing being removed. *My nerves are really shot. It's a good thing I don't have to take any pictures right now. They'd be nothing but a blur.*

A few minutes later Leslie was lying as close to the edge of the sleeping bag as possible, the darkness still penetrated by flashes from the lightning storm in spite of the cover Duke had put over the window. She tried her best to relax and go to sleep. Duke had seemed especially tactful about the whole process of getting into bed, not making any suggestive comments or seductive moves. Now he was lying quietly, his back turned to her. For all she knew, he was already asleep. She closed her eyes, deliberately relaxing muscles that were tied in tense knots, listening intently to the music in an attempt to decrease her painful awareness of the large warm male body only inches away from hers. Very slowly she succeeded, her mind beginning to wander aimlessly, music and mental images melting together and fading away. Then, as if she had been thrust into the very center of a bursting skyrocket, there was a flash that seemed to be both inside and outside her closed eyelids. Her whole body jerked upright, and she let out a scream of anguish.

"Leslie, what is it?" Duke cried, his arms reaching toward her.

CHAPTER FIVE

"HE'S GONE! He's gone! My God, he's gone!" Leslie sobbed, collapsing into the arms that pulled her close.

"Who is gone? What happened, little one? A nightmare?" Duke held Leslie tightly, stroking her hair comfortingly as she continued to sob uncontrollably.

"Oh, Lord," Leslie breathed, her heart still pounding and her body trembling as she as last sensed where she was. "It's not real again. I'm here. Thank God."

"What—" Duke began, then interrupted himself. "I'd better turn on the light. You'll feel better." In a flash he had done so and then gathered Leslie into his arms again. "Want to tell me about it?" he asked softly as Leslie gladly burrowed into the welcome protection of his strong arms. When she did not reply but only nodded against his chest, he asked, "Is it a recurring dream about something that really happened to you?"

"Yes," Leslie replied hoarsely. "I was in Beirut on an assignment to take pictures of the day-to-day life of children caught in the midst of a war. I was watching a little boy playing with a toy truck on the edges of a ruined building. I had my camera focused on him, and then...a bomb exploded—" She could say no more, and Duke's arms tightened around her, his lips nuzzling her cheek.

"Shhh," he whispered. "I understand. Try not to think about it now."

"I can't help it," Leslie sobbed.

"Yes, you can." He laid her back against his shoulder and looked at her sternly. "You must. I had a...similar experience in Vietnam. Such things burn themselves into your memory, but you have to push them aside, think about other things, or they can take over your life. It's hard at first, but it gets easier." He smiled gently then and wiped the tears from Leslie's cheeks with his thumb. "Lightning must have struck close by. It woke me up, too. Want to stay awake a while and talk?"

"What about?" Leslie asked, the horrifying images of minutes ago giving way to a feeling of warmth and security that seemed to flow from the strong shoulder against which she lay and the kindness she saw in the beautiful dark eyes so close to hers.

"Well, let's see..." Duke's eyebrows met in a thoughtful frown. "I'd like to know more about this lovely, mysterious lady who appeared like a genie one night in my truck. How about telling me about your family? Where did you grow up?"

She wasn't sure if he really wanted to hear all that, but he did know how to distract her, Leslie thought gratefully, smiling back as Duke smiled at her encouragingly.

"I was almost born backstage at the Metropolitan Opera House," she said, chuckling as Duke raised his eyebrows in exaggerated surprise. "My father is a violinist, and he was playing with the Met orchestra then." She went on to tell of her family's frequent moves as her father took succeedingly better jobs, finally becoming concertmaster of a famous orchestra. Interspersed with her tales of the happy memories she had of her younger brother and sister and the chaos of the piano lessons that her mother gave in their home, she encouraged Duke to talk a little about his childhood. It disturbed her that, in spite of what sounded like a relatively happy and certainly privileged childhood, he still had nothing positive to say about his mother. In fact, he never mentioned her at all. She knew that this was not the time to bring up the subject, but she vowed privately that, somehow, someday, she would bring them together.

At last Leslie grew drowsy, her eyelids heavy.

"Go ahead, shut your eyes," Duke said softly.

He drew his hand slowly down across her face, and she fell asleep almost instantly and was unaware that, while she slept nestled in his arms, Duke lay awake for a long time, feeling more disturbed than he could ever remember by the presence of a beautiful woman in his bed.

"I BEG YOUR PARDON."

Leslie's eyes flew open, and she let out a little gasp as she saw Duke crouched above her, his chin and jaw dark with stubble and his eyes tired and red-looking.

"There's only one way out of this bed," he said gruffly as he looked quickly away and climbed on over her. "Just turn over and go back to sleep. I can't sleep, so I thought I might as well get rolling."

In a flash the events of the night came back to Leslie. Poor Duke. She had interrupted his sleep and then kept him awake for ages talking. He looked exhausted.

"I'm sorry if I bothered you," she said, turning away as commanded. "Thank you for—for being so understanding."

"Don't mention it," Duke replied brusquely. "I'd do the same for anyone with that kind of problem."

Leslie frowned. What was he implying? That she thought she held some special place in his affections? That was a laugh!

"I rather assumed that you would," she said tightly.

She lay quietly thinking, as the sounds of Duke preparing for the day went on. Maybe, she thought, if they were getting an especially early start, Duke hoped to shake the ubiquitous Mr. Callahan and be able to leave her in St. Louis. If so, she had better get ready herself. Discerning that Duke was dressed by now, she turned back over and looked at him.

"Are you going to drop me off in St. Louis?" she asked as he cast a brief glance at her.

He shrugged and inspected his face in a small mirror on one of the cabinet doors.

"That, Miss Lyon," he said, "depends entirely on what Callahan does. If he is nowhere in sight, I may. Otherwise, I certainly will not."

"If we leave right away, he may not even realize we're gone for a long time," Leslie said, swinging her feet to the floor and sitting on the edge of the bunk.

Duke made an unpleasant snorting sound. "If you think I'm going to start right out without any coffee or breakfast, think again. I'd probably doze off and have us in a ditch within five miles."

Leslie's heart sank. "But . . . Callahan may hear you or see you going to the restaurant," she said. "Couldn't you—"

"No!"

Duke scowled, more fiercely, Leslie thought, than the occasion warranted. He was certainly in a foul mood. His face, she noticed, was pale and lined-looking now that it was clean shaven, as if he had slept hardly at all.

She pursed her mouth and looked down, realizing it was futile to argue.

"And don't sit there looking like a—like a disgruntled pink rabbit," he added, a slightly softer edge to his voice. "I have enough on my mind already."

Leslie looked back at him, surprised, but he had turned away and was putting on a leather jacket. Without another word he pushed his way through the opening into the cab of the truck. Then his head reappeared.

"Keep quiet, and keep the doors locked," he hissed. "Callahan's already up."

"Oh, shut up!" Leslie snapped as his head disappeared again. What did he think she was going to do? Throw herself from the frying pan into the fire? She flung herself back against the pillows. That she felt disgruntled was putting it mildly. She was ready to scream and throw things in frustration. Maybe she had hoped that his kindness last night had meant that he felt something more for her than alternating lust and contempt. But maybe all that it had meant was that he was curious about her as some kind of sexual oddity, and while he respected her values, she was, so to speak, out of the game as far as he was concerned.

Well, that was just fine with her. Just perfectly fine! Let him spend his life with women who were willing to take what they could get for a few of his dazzling smiles and adorable winks, and then wake up in the morning to find that he had gone. Let him spend his life thinking his mother hated him when she probably adored him. There wasn't much that Leslie Lyon could do about it. There wasn't much she could do about anything!

Leslie jumped to her feet and drove her fist into her palm. The whole situation was getting to her more all the time. She was sick and tired of feeling so helpless. No wonder caged animals paced endlessly back and forth. She felt as if she might explode if she could not soon take control of her own life again. But how could she, when two men, neither of whom had any reason at all to want her caged, nevertheless were determined to keep her there?

Suddenly she stopped her pacing and frowned. How did she know that Callahan was really a villain? All she had was Duke's word for it. She had never even seen the man. She had heard the few words he'd spoken, but they could be taken two ways. Maybe he really wanted to help her! Maybe he thought Duke was the villain! She quickly grabbed her slacks and sweater. It was time to get out of this darned truck and find out. She would go into the restaurant, and if Callahan showed up, she'd talk to him. To hell with what Duke wanted her to do. She was fed up with his mistrust of her.

In minutes Leslie was dressed and zipping up her jacket. Darn! She couldn't get her camera bag, and it had all of her identification in it. Well, she'd deal with that later. She bent to unzip the opening and then froze. Outside there was the sound of heavy footsteps coming closer and then sounding on the steps of the truck. Someone tried the door, shaking it vigorously. Then there was a tapping on the window.

"Hey, little cutie pie," a voice called out. "Come on out. I know you're in there. Ain't you gettin' tired of Caldwell by now? I can show you what a real man is like."

Leslie sank down on the floor of the sleeper and buried her face in her hands. Oh, God, she had almost done it again! What had she been thinking of? She had known all along that Duke hadn't lied to her. But she'd felt so trapped, so desperate. What if she had blundered out and that man had grabbed her? Her stomach churned at the thought. His was neither the voice nor the words of a person she wanted to meet, let alone exchange Duke Caldwell for.

"You ain't gonna have much more time with Caldwell, ya know," the voice went on. "He's a rich guy, not a real trucker. He'll dump you as soon as you hit California. Me, I'd take you home with me. I could use something pretty like you around the house."

She could imagine what for, Leslie thought, shuddering. She sat as still as death, first praying for Duke's quick return and then for Callahan to be gone before Duke got back. There might be a fight if Duke caught him there, and she would not be surprised if Callahan was good with his fists. He might even carry a gun. To her relief, she presently heard the man climb back down the steps and walk away. Apparently he had no desire to confront Duke.

Leslie got up and quietly took off her jacket and the rest of her clothes, and put on the black warm-up suit, smiling grimly at the row of ducks on her shirt. "No," she muttered to them, "everything is not just ducky. Not by a long shot." She put some water and detergent into the washbasin and rinsed out her underwear. Might as well settle in for a long siege. She would stick with Duke to Timbuktu before she would get out of the truck if Callahan was anywhere nearby.

Duke reappeared just as Leslie was squeezing the excess moisture from her undergarments, which she'd rolled in a thick towel.

"Have a nice chat with Callahan?" he asked, tossing a paper bag onto the counter and setting a thermos beside it. His expression was stony as he cast a sideways glance at Leslie.

Leslie stared at him, feeling a venomous rage begin to boil in her already-tense body. This was it! She had had all the nonsense she could take! She took a wild swing at Duke with the rolled-up towel.

"You idiot!" she shouted. "You moron! How could you possibly think that I would have anything to do with that—that vulgar degenerate! You are the stupidest, most stubborn, most imperceptive man on the face of the earth! If you saw him, why didn't you make him go away? He said disgusting things, and he scared me. I didn't say anything. Not anything at all!"

She struggled and swung viciously with her other hand as Duke grabbed the towel-bearing one and tried to dance away from Leslie's kicking feet. "Let me go!" she cried as he finally pinned both of her arms to her sides. "Don't touch me! I don't want you near me if you think that of me. Let me go!" she repeated, half sobbing, as Duke's arms went around her and he held her tightly against his chest with a steely grip.

His entire body felt as tense and hard and cold as iron. Then suddenly he shuddered, as if with a terrible chill, and his grip became gentle, his body warm and yielding. One hand reached beneath her hair and caressed her neck and shoulders soothingly. Leslie could feel the pressure of his cheek as he laid his head against her hair.

"I don't think that," he said huskily. "I haven't for some time. I'm sorry if he frightened you."

"Then why did you keep pretending you did?" Leslie cried. She looked up and met Duke's eyes, which were now deep dark pools of gentle concern. "Why?" she repeated.

"Because," Duke replied, caressing her cheek with his thumb, "I wanted to keep you here without frightening you unduly." He smiled crookedly. "I didn't think you were particularly afraid of me. As it is, I don't know why Callahan is following us or what he wants, but the ideas that come to mind aren't very pleasant. And—" his face became very sober "—I still don't plan to let you go until I do know."

Leslie took a deep, unsteady breath. Duke's confession that he no longer thought she was here on some guilty mission left her feeling weak with relief; the warmth of his closeness was so comforting. She closed her eyes and buried her face against his massive chest again. "Don't worry," she said hoarsely, "I don't want to go anywhere until we do." She paused. "Couldn't you just tell the police about him?"

Duke shook his head. "So far the man hasn't done anything illegal. I wish to hell he would. But truckers often stick together on long hauls, and since we're both going to approximately the same place, he could just say he wanted company. You can't hang a man for that."

"Oh, dear," Leslie chewed her lip. "This is all my fault. If only I'd stayed in New York, none of this would have happened. Why don't I ever learn—" She stopped as Duke lifted her face between his hands and smiled down at her whimsically.

"Poor little green-eyed pussycat. Are you really sorry you stowed away, or do you just wish it had turned out differently?"

"Well..." Leslie tried to look away, but Duke ducked his head and followed her eyes so that she was forced to look into his. She felt so confused with him staring at her like that, as if he were reading her thoughts before she even spoke. "I—I thought you probably wished you'd never set eyes on me," she stammered. "Half the time you've acted as if you hated me."

Duke tilted his head and put on a comically perplexed look. "Was there an answer to my question in there somewhere? If there was, I missed it, but never mind. I think I know the answer. And in case you were asking, I'm not at all sorry you stowed away, except for the problems of Callahan, which we'll cope with somehow. You are a fascinating woman, Leslie Lyon. Confusing, but fascinating." He shook his head with that same bemused look, then quite suddenly lowered his mouth to Leslie's.

Startled, Leslie stood still for a moment, her arms at her sides. Then, as her own mouth responded like a flower opening to the sun, her arms stole around Duke's broad back, and she pulled him fiercely against her. In turn he responded with thrusts of his tongue that sent currents of excitement from its tip to her inner lips, her cheeks, her own tongue. As if it were like a game of tag, they tasted and played together in wild patterns of movement. Leslie's heart was pounding, and her head was whirling. She felt like crying and laughing and shouting all at once.

If Duke is confused, she thought as she hooked one arm upward and felt his strong shoulder with her hand, *then what on earth am I?* When he tried to move away, she held him even more tightly, then stared at him, dazed, as he drew his head back, closed his mouth and appeared to swallow hard.

"I think I'd better start driving," he said hoarsely.

"I suppose so," Leslie answered, her own voice none too steady. She was still standing in the circle of his arms.

Duke's eyes remained fixed on hers. "There are coffee and doughnuts over there." He jerked his head toward the little countertop.

Leslie nodded. "Thank you." She could not tear her eyes from Duke's. As if magnetized, they continued to stare at each other. Finally Duke shook his head and blinked.

"That could be habit-forming," he said wryly. He gave Leslie a wink. "You'd better keep it under lock and key."

Leslie watched as Duke's massive shoulders disappeared through the opening into the driver's compartment. She still felt confused to the point of dizziness, but she felt something else too, she thought, something new, unlike anything she had ever felt before. A lightness. It was almost as if she could float on air, like one of those tiny seeds from a dandelion with its little sail of fluff. Was it Duke's kiss that had set her flying? His revelation that he no longer suspected her of any subterfuge? Or was it because Duke hadn't scolded her for her temper or let her blame herself for the mess she had gotten both of them into? She had never met a man like him before, a man who seemed to have so quickly learned the nuances of her character and how to cope with them. Gentleness, firmness, humor. He was so good with all of them. He would be, she thought wistfully, so easy to love.

"Oh, my," Leslie breathed, her hand going to cover her mouth. Was that it? Was she falling in love with Duke Caldwell?

CHAPTER SIX

LESLIE STAGGERED and clutched at the countertop for support, not sure whether it was the shock of the idea or the fact that the truck was now underway that made her unsteady. She turned up to the small mirror that Duke had looked into earlier, half expecting to find some answer written on her face. She did look unusually pink-cheeked and bright-eyed, but then, she looked that way after a brisk walk on a windy day.

I can't be, she thought. *It's too soon. Too much has happened to me.* Besides, Duke didn't believe in the kind of love she believed in, or marriage, either, and with his background and at his age, it would probably be one devil of a job to convince him otherwise. One of her mother's favorite maxims had been: Don't ever think you can change a man. If you can't take him the way he is, leave him alone. The application in the present situation was obvious. Mrs. Lyon's daughter had better not be in love with Duke Caldwell.

At the sound of Duke's voice, she turned away from the mirror. "You're awfully quiet back there. Are you all right?" he asked.

"I'm fine," Leslie answered, thinking grimly, *Oh, sure I am.* Something inside her had melted at the deep, husky tones that had become so familiar.

"Have you tried those doughnuts yet? I got the jelly-filled kind this time. I hope you like them."

"Love them," Leslie replied quickly. "I was just about to have one." Oh, dear, if he was going to be nice to her all the time now... Probably the only thing that had kept her from falling head over heels, hopelessly in love with the man from that first adorable wink had been his hostility and suspicion in thinking she was a hired temptress. With a sigh Leslie took out a doughnut, poured herself a cup of coffee and sat down on the edge of the bunk to meditate on her new predicament.

What she needed, she decided shortly, was some time away from Duke Caldwell to think things over. Maybe this wasn't love at all but another manifestation of her tendency to plunge headlong where angels feared to tread. If only Callahan would go away so that she could get out in St. Louis.

"Is Callahan still following us?" she asked.

"I'm afraid so," Duke answered. He was silent for a minute. "If you're worried about missing your appointment in St. Louis, don't be. If we haven't resolved this by Sunday afternoon, we'll park the rig, and I'll fly back to St. Louis with you to make sure he doesn't bother you. Then if he should come after you, we'd have plenty of cause to call the authorities in."

Leslie shuddered. Apparently Duke was thinking along the same lines as she had been about Mr. Callahan's possible motivation. But that would only mean more inconvenience for Duke. She knew he found her attractive—he'd even called her fascinating—but she doubted he was anxious to bring his own life to a halt while he looked after her. He had a load to deliver, a job to attend to. Surely, once she was in the air, she'd be safe.

"You don't need to interrupt your trip," she said. "I don't think he'd follow me by air."

"I wasn't asking for your opinion," Duke said sharply. "We take no chances."

"Well, aren't *we* bossy," Leslie snapped back.

Duke chuckled. "Only to forestall an argument on a topic upon which there is no room for discussion," he said.

"And why isn't there?"

"Because I'm damned if I want to be worried about you. It would be far less bother to come with you."

"Oh." Leslie chewed her lip. For a moment she had thought that perhaps Duke was revealing an unpleasant trait, but his last speech had scotched that notion. He obviously cared what happened to her. Of course, he'd probably do the same for anyone under the circumstances, she reminded herself. Still, things might change by Sunday. Was that tomorrow? She was no longer quite sure what day it was.

"Is today Saturday?" she asked. "I've lost track of time."

"Saturday it is. And in case you're curious, we'll be heading south out of St. Louis, pick up Interstate 40 west of Memphis, go across Arkansas and be in Texas tomorrow. We can leave from the Dallas-Fort Worth Airport if necessary. Okay?"

"Sounds terrific," Leslie said with a sigh. She cleaned up after her breakfast, then sat back against the bunk pillows, trying to read but feeling too unsettled to do so. Something was bothering her, and she was not quite sure what it was. Goodness knew, there were plenty of possibilities! Callahan's pursuit. Her feelings toward Duke. His feelings—if there were any special ones—toward her.

A wailing noise interrupted Leslie's meditations, first only adding to her thoughts and then capturing her attention completely as it grew louder. That was what had been niggling in her mind, almost forgotten for a time—the message she'd left on the washroom wall and now...its results. A siren! The police had caught up with them at last!

My God, what shall I do? Leslie thought in desperation. She did not want Duke arrested now. Could she tell the police it had been a mistake? Would they believe her? Or would they think she was under duress and lying because he had threatened her? Would Duke be handcuffed, dragged to the nearest police station and questioned? She could imagine his stony silence, his anger, even though, at the time she left her message, she'd had good reason to do so. How glad he would be to be rid of one Leslie Lyon when the ordeal was over!

As the siren drew near, Leslie climbed up and pushed aside the plastic cover Duke had put over the window, just enough so that she could peer out. She watched for the approaching police car with all the enthusiasm of a person waiting to go to the gallows. Soon she could see flashing lights, then the speeding car came alongside the truck...and then sped by as if pursuing the devil himself, a long black limousine flying in its wake.

The sound of Duke's hearty laugh came over the intercom. "That was the old Eagle-1, still trying to get somewhere without taking to the skies. He's probably late for a luncheon talk in St. Louis."

"That was—Loren Barstow?" Leslie croaked hoarsely as she sank weakly onto the bunk.

"The same," Duke affirmed, still chuckling. "The old rascal doesn't mind doing close to a hundred miles an hour as long as he's still on the ground and has a police escort."

Leslie shook her head, her stomach still feeling queasy. What if what she had feared had happened...? Somehow, before it did, she had to get to a telephone and make the authorities believe that her message had been only the result of a temporary misunderstanding. She just had to!

But in spite of her fervent prayers, they skirted St. Louis and headed south toward Memphis, and lunchtime came and went with no opportunity presenting itself. Duke was only out of the truck long enough to refuel, and although Leslie thought it quite likely that she could persuade him to let her get out if she stayed close by, she had no desire to subject herself to the leers and comments of Callahan. He had stopped at the same place they had, his determination to be their shadow apparently undiminished. Her frustration made Leslie lapse into uncommunicative silence as she and Duke ate the sandwiches she had prepared.

"Something bothering you besides being cooped up for so long?" Duke asked.

"Oh...no," Leslie replied, trying to perk up and look more pleasant. It was difficult while every minute she worried about the possibility of a patrol car looming into view. And it was also difficult now that she was no longer a suspect and she felt free to take Duke at face value, admiring both his warm personality and the physical attractiveness that made her as giddy as a teenager. What was she going to do about that? What could she do? Would she ever see Duke again, once they were free of Callahan's presence?

"Are you worried about coming up with the money to pay for your sister's car?" Duke inquired next. "Because if you are, I can make you a loan. I'm damned flattered that you thought I'd do for that Fling promotion, and since I can't take the job..."

Leslie shook her head quickly. "I couldn't let you do that," she said. "I'm not in any financial difficulty. If necessary I can get a regular loan, but I shouldn't have to if I can get a few extra jobs." She grinned suddenly, wondering if Duke thought she was used to scrimping. "I demand quite a large fee for my work these days."

"How large?" Duke asked, cocking an eyebrow at her.

"That depends on the job—how difficult or time-consuming it is. Why?"

"Because I may have a job that might interest you," Duke replied. "I'm going to need some publicity photos for the political campaign next fall. Think you could do that sort of thing?"

"Of course I could!" Leslie cried, feeling suddenly like turning handsprings. Duke didn't want to get rid of her immediately! "I'd love to do it. But I wouldn't want to charge you for it. I'm anxious for you to win that election, too. You can consider it a campaign contribution."

"No way," Duke replied with a firm shake of his head. "I insist on paying your regular fee. If you want to make a contribution—a small one—you may do it through regular channels." He laughed as Leslie's face fell.

"What's so funny?" she demanded.

"I was just thinking how far we've come from our initial misunderstanding," he replied with a gentle smile. "Now if I can just convince you that there is more than one way for a man and woman to have a rewarding relationship, we'll have come all the way."

Leslie stared at him openmouthed, a strange quivering in the pit of her stomach. Duke was confessing to feeling a strong attraction for her, something more than a physical turn-on. But what was he suggesting? That they have an affair? She hadn't expected that! Last night he had seemed so—so understanding of her viewpoint, so restrained.

"Don't look so surprised," he said with a teasing wink. "Why do you suppose I had such a hard time keeping my mind on the fact that you were the villainous Miss Leslie Lyon, the despicable wench set on destroying my pristine reputation? Have you any idea how glad I was to finally believe you weren't? I was almost ready to say to hell with it, I didn't really give a damn what intentions you had. It was partly the confusion between what I believed and what I wanted to believe that kept me from letting you know sooner. I didn't trust myself." As Leslie continued to stare, her cheeks pink and her eyes wide, he bent toward her. "Good heavens, Leslie, don't you know when a man is attracted to you? Do you think I kiss everyone like that? Even a man with considerable practice can't fake desire that well."

"I'm...not sure what I think," Leslie replied, swallowing hard. "You know that I'm not...I don't..." She stumbled to a halt as Duke bent his head close.

"Of course," he said softly. "I just said I did. And I don't intend to take any kind of advantage of you or put undue pressure on you. However, I do intend to make it clear to you how much pleasure and happiness you'll be missing if you keep to your archaic values."

"H-how?" Leslie stammered. She was scarcely able to breathe, staring entranced into the deep, soft darkness of Duke's eyes.

"Like this," he replied, one arm going around behind Leslie's neck as he touched his lips to hers, first delicately and then with increasing pressure as she responded. "There," he said moments later, withdrawing a few inches and smiling at her. "Lesson number one. Now as much as I'd prefer continuing your education, I'm afraid I must return to driving this rig."

Leslie shook her head to try to clear it. If that wasn't undue pressure! "I don't need educating," she said, frowning as Duke got to his feet.

"Oh, I think you do. I think the only reason you've been able to cling to that Louisa May Alcott mentality of yours is that no man has aroused you enough either physically or mentally to make you have second thoughts. I intend to give you plenty to think about." He grinned as Leslie's frown darkened. "I don't expect you to immediately welcome the opportunity," he said teasingly.

"You certainly flatter yourself if you think you're the first man who's tried to convince me I was old-fashioned," she said.

"I didn't think I was," Duke replied cheerfully with another of his mischievous winks, just before he disappeared through the doorway.

Leslie stared after him, trying hard to think of some fitting put-down but coming up with nothing. This sudden turnabout had her completely confused. Was Duke simply challenged by her virginity? Did he want to add her to what was probably a long list of women with whom he had had "meaningful" but brief relationships? Whatever his motivation, she had better get her guard up and keep it there! He must be well aware how close she had been to abandoning herself to him only yesterday. And now that she knew him better, she didn't find him any less attractive. Add that to her impetuous streak, and she could easily find herself in more trouble than she cared to think about.

With a sigh she got up and put away the luncheon ingredients and tidied up the little space. *Come on, Leslie, be honest,* she told herself. Duke Caldwell had been hard enough to resist when she was furious with him. Could she keep her resolve now that he was determined to break it down? She had to. She had always planned that when she gave herself to a man, it would be because her heart and soul were his, too, for always, an idea that Duke scorned. Now was a really good time to pay attention to her mother's advice.

What's the matter, Leslie? an insidious little voice seemed to whisper in her ear. *Are you afraid you're going to give in? You always think of your mother when you're in trouble.*

I am not! Leslie retorted to her imaginary adversary. *I'm just being practical.* The problem was that Duke Caldwell didn't believe in love and marriage and probably never would, and as soon as he found out she really wouldn't give in, he'd drop her like poison, and that would be that. He was certainly not the type to pursue an unwilling woman all over the country, begging for her favors. And she was not going to give in. She was going to stop that little "education" program of his before it went any further by letting him know in as many ways as possible that it wouldn't work. So there!

Lots of luck, the voice whispered. *You're going to need it.*

"Oh, shush!" Leslie said aloud and flung herself down on the bunk.

"What did you say?" Duke asked.

"Nothing," Leslie replied quickly, rubbing her forehead to try to clear her muddled mind. She had better get that mind on something else before she got any more confused. She had thought it was bad being Duke's physical prisoner, but it seemed as if one problem had just been exchanged for another even more complex one. Maybe if she wrote down everything that had happened since she started on this escapade, it might help her to get things in better perspective.

"Are there any writing materials in here?" she asked.

"In the drawer below the basin," Duke replied. "What are you going to write?"

"Kind of a retroactive diary," Leslie replied. "I'm afraid I'll never be able to remember everything that's happened in the past few days otherwise. I want to be able to tell my grandchildren about it someday." She cocked an ear, waiting for Duke's reply. Grandchildren were obviously not something he was planning on, and it wouldn't do her cause any harm to let him know that she was.

Duke chuckled as if he saw through her ploy. "Aren't you a little young to be thinking about grandchildren? It might be more to the point to write a story. If you change the names to protect its innocent participants—"

"You're not so innocent," Leslie retorted, ignoring his reference to the grandchildren issue. "If you knew I was in here from the beginning, why didn't you just stop the truck and throw me out before we left New York? It would have saved both of us a great deal of trouble. By the way, how did you know I was here?"

"You jumped a foot when those apples landed on you," Duke replied. "I figured it must be that cute little redhead who wanted to talk to me, and I was too curious about what you had in mind to throw you out."

"Oh, so Tony was right," Leslie said. "You were hoping for a little extra fun on your trip."

"No, that is not what I thought!" Duke exclaimed, his voice harsh. "My first impression of you was not of a woman who would— You know. It wasn't until I put together your appearance, your cameras and Callahan that I suspected something. I simply wanted to know what was so important that you'd go so far as to stow away in my truck in order to talk to me."

My goodness, Leslie thought, how anxious Duke was now to try to undo the results of his accusations!

"Well, at least your first hunch was right," she said quickly. "What if I'd popped out when Tony was still with you? I almost did, but I was scared by the way he looked and acted. He seemed almost as bad as Callahan."

"Tony? He's a good guy," Duke said, his voice returning to normal. "He wouldn't have bothered you. And if you'd made your pitch for the Fling business before I met up with Callahan, I'd probably have believed you, given you a polite no and sent you on your way. Aren't you glad now that you procrastinated?"

"Good heavens, but you have a colossal ego!" Leslie cried. "Do you actually think I'm delighted to have spent forty-eight hours cooped up in this sleeper? Think again!"

"You said you wanted to write it all down," Duke replied calmly. "If it's been so miserable, why not forget it?"

"I am simply trying to make the best of things," Leslie snapped coldly, although she smiled wryly to herself as she did so. Duke was certainly determined to pursue her "education" program, even from a distance, trying to get her to admit to being so attracted to him that she actually enjoyed her captivity. Or was he only trying to relieve some of the guilt he doubtless felt? Leslie shrugged to herself. Whatever the reason, she wasn't about to give him the satisfaction of knowing that he was at least partly right. The farther she kept him at bay, the better. So far the only indication of his filings-to-a-magnet attraction for her had been in her physical response to him. Well, that was all he was going to get, and she had better make sure there wasn't any more of that. It was too dangerous for her sanity—and for her resolve. But she would definitely have to stay on her toes. He was pretty clever. It would probably be best to stay on the offensive herself, whenever she could.

With that in mind, she quickly asked, "Why don't you let me come up in the cab with you now? Does it matter if Callahan sees me since he seems to be sure I'm here, anyway?"

Duke was silent for a few moments. "I don't think you'd better," he replied. "Sorry," he added as Leslie groaned. "We still don't know what Callahan has in mind. He may be after you for some unpleasant reason, or he might still just want to see that you are here in order to be able to carry the tale to his boss or someone connected with Phillips's campaign. They might pay him something, even if all he comes up with is a good story, one that he might be able to produce some additional witnesses to. Which is, of course, another problem. The farther west we get, the more likely we are to encounter someone else I know, and I wouldn't like to have to come up with some lame explanation for your being here."

Leslie's temper flared. "Oh, so I'm still a prisoner here, all because of your precious reputation! But suddenly I've become eligible for your sexual advances. How very interesting. Well, let me tell you something, Duke Caldwell, you have about as much chance of 'educating' me as you do of teaching a gorilla to fly! I want no part of any of your tawdry, cheap, sneaky relationships. My, how careful you must have to be to keep your Sir Lancelot image. It would almost be fun to unmask you. You're just damned lucky that I have a reputation to protect myself, one which, I might point out, I come by honestly."

Duke whistled softly. "You *are* fed up with being stuck in that sleeper," he said. "I don't blame you a bit. But it will only be until tomorrow, at worst, so try to look on the bright side."

"What bright side?" Leslie snapped.

"You've met me," Duke replied and then roared with laughter as Leslie uttered several unladylike expletives.

"And another thing," he added shortly. "You seem to have discretion confused with some less apt descriptions of the kind of relationship I have in mind. I don't keep my women friends locked away in a mountain cabin, or even in a penthouse. Since they are usually either socially prominent or talented professional women like yourself, that idea is ridiculous. We do the usual things that men and women who enjoy each other's company do. We go out together, go to the finest restaurants, the theater, sporting events. And sometimes on cruises on private yachts, or skiing in the Alps. I even have a friend who owns an entire island in the South Pacific that we visit from time to time. The only difference from what you have in mind is that neither of us owns the other or makes demands that can't be met.

We're free to see others if we want, or to stop seeing each other if it seems appropriate. Does that sound like anything sleazy?''

Leslie shook her head silently, then scowled. Duke's words conjured up images of suntanned women in elegant gowns, hanging on his arm or stretched out full-length beside his own long bare body on the deck of a huge yacht. Just the thought of those women gave her a gnawing pain, but she was not up for that kind of life. Not Leslie Lyon, the hardworking, ambitious daughter of honest, hardworking people.

"Revising your notions?" Duke interrupted her reverie.

"I'm afraid not," Leslie replied. "I've seen the beautiful people at play, and I'm not one of them, nor do I want to be. You'd better cross me off your list." She bit her lip. *And I'd better cross you off mine,* she added to herself. There was no way in the world that a man used to that kind of life was going to suddenly settle down. Why did it hurt so much to face that fact? She'd known it all along.

"Oh . . . rats!" she muttered.

"You can say that again," Duke said. "There's a patrol car coming up on me, and he's signaling me to pull over. I wonder what in hell he wants?"

CHAPTER SEVEN

"OH, MY GOD!" Leslie cried inadvertently.

"Don't panic, Leslie," Duke said gruffly. "I'll handle it. Just stay put. It can't be anything serious."

That's what you think! Leslie thought grimly, grabbing her regular clothing and getting into everything in record time. Duke had just pulled over to the side of the road and opened his door when she slipped into her jacket and unzipped the door to the truck's cab. She had no clear plan as to what she would do or say. She only knew that she must somehow make it clear that Duke Caldwell was not abducting her.

"Let me see your driver's license," she heard a voice say as Duke swung himself to the ground.

"What's the problem, officer?" Duke's voice inquired calmly.

Leslie wished she could have been fast enough to have seen Duke's face at the patrolman's next words.

"We have a report here that a woman named Leslie Lyon may be being held captive in a Buena Suerte Farms truck," the man said. "I think we'd better take a look—"

What Leslie did see was the officer's startled expression when he looked up and saw her descending the truck steps, and then Duke's equally amazed look as he turned toward her.

"I'm Leslie Lyon," she said before Duke could speak. "I'm sorry about the misunderstanding, but I left that message before...before I knew why Duke was taking me on this trip."

The officer and his partner, who had joined him, inspected Leslie closely. *Oh dear,* she thought as they then looked at Duke even more suspiciously. *I must look like something the cat dragged in!*

"And just why did you take her, apparently against her will?" the first officer asked, fixing Duke with a steely glare. "Don't you know there are laws against transporting women for immoral purposes?"

Oh, good Lord, Leslie thought in a panic as Duke turned as red as a boiled lobster and stayed just as silent.

"It wasn't that at all!" she cried quickly, and as the officer returned his gaze to her, she blurted out, "Duke and I have been...going together for almost a year, and he kept asking me to marry him, but I couldn't make up my mind between him and another man in New York. So he just picked me up and took me away and told me he was going to be the one." She paused, breathless, and made a stab at smiling and batting her lashes at Duke. "At first I was really mad at him, but I'm not anymore. We're going to be married in June." She gave the officer her best wide-eyed innocent look. "That isn't immoral, is it?"

The officer eyed Leslie skeptically.

"Is that true?" he asked Duke.

Leslie stared in fascination at the play of expressions on Duke's face as he looked down at her, as if he were not sure whether he wanted to kill her or congratulate her. He was so slow in answering that she was afraid the officer would doubt whatever he said, but at last he nodded.

"It is," he replied.

"Well, we'll have to take some statements from both of you," the second officer was beginning to say when suddenly a long, black, chauffeur-driven limousine screeched to a stop in front of the parked truck and police cars, backed up along the shoulder and discharged a tall, thin, distinguished-looking man.

"Who the hell is that?" the first officer asked the second.

"I dunno. Oh, hey, it's that lawyer fellow, isn't it? The one who was supposed to talk in St. Louis today to the governor's task force on crime?"

"Yeah, that's him all right. I wonder what he wants?" said the first officer.

"My God, it's Loren Barstow," Duke and Leslie said in unison.

"Duke! Leslie!" cried the barrister in his famous booming voice, coming toward them with his arms outstretched, his appearance dramatic as usual. "Here I am, on my way to Memphis, and I find two of my favorite people confronting the law on this lonely road without my help." He gave the patrolmen a charming smile and extended his hand to each of them. "I'm Loren Barstow," he said, sure of their recognition of that famous name. "What are these nefarious characters up to?"

"You know these people?" the officer asked.

Barstow replied with a booming, "I certainly do." Leslie saw Duke flinch visibly as he went on, "This is Duke Caldwell, the future congressman from California, and Miss Leslie Lyon, the world-famous photographer."

At that revelation the patrolmen took Loren Barstow aside and talked to him in low tones for several minutes.

While they conversed, Leslie tugged on Duke's sleeve and stood on tiptoe to whisper in his ear. "It might be more convincing if you'd put your arm around me."

Duke cocked an eyebrow at Leslie and gave her a wry smile but did as she suggested just as Loren Barstow whirled, his face wearing that wondrous smile that was frequently described as being capable of convincing juries that black was white.

"Duke, my boy, congratulations!" he cried, grabbing Duke's hand and pumping it furiously. "I was wondering when you were going to stop spreading your largess and settle down. My God, man, you couldn't have picked a better woman. Leslie, my love—" he gave her a huge hug and a resounding kiss "—you are the perfect woman for this man, and you've found yourself one of the best." He backed off a step and beamed at them. "This is one of the nicest surprises I've ever had," he boomed. "When's the happy day?"

"Uh, sometime in June, although we haven't set the date exactly," Leslie said quickly, giving Duke a feeble smile. "We haven't even had time to tell our families yet."

"Ah, I see," Loren Barstow said with a conspiratorial wink at them. "This mad escapade isn't over yet. Well, I won't breathe a word for a while. Give you time to get everything set. You be sure to let me know, though, because I want a front-row seat at the wedding."

"You'll get that, all right," Duke said, finally moved to say a few words. He gestured at the patrolmen. "Is there any way we can straighten out this...mis-understanding without it taking all day?''

"No problem," Loren boomed, "no problem at all. I'll handle it for you." He turned to the officers and spoke to them rapidly for several minutes. They soon nodded and smiled agreeably and retreated to their car after politely shaking Duke and Leslie's hands and wishing them well.

"There we are," said Loren Barstow, beaming broadly. "All set. There may be some papers for you to sign, but I'll be in touch. Just don't leave the earth," he joked. "Well, this is splendid, just splendid. I'd like to hear more of your story, but I've got to be in Memphis in a couple of hours for a talk to the bar association, so you two take care. And my blessings on you both." He shook Duke's hand again, kissed Leslie enthusiastically and returned to his limousine, waving out the back as it sped away.

Leslie stood stock-still, staring after the departing limousine, not so much fascinated with the sight as she was afraid to look at Duke, who was still uncharacteristically silent. Finally she looked up at him, and he raised his eyebrows at her, deep flickering sparks of some undetermined nature in his eyes sending tremors through her. What was he thinking? she wondered. Doubtless she would soon find out.

"Let's go," he said as he propelled Leslie ahead of him up the steps of the truck cab.

Instead of retreating into the sleeper, Leslie sat down on the passenger seat.

"Go into the back," Duke ordered brusquely.

Leslie scowled. "Why should I? Callahan's gone now, isn't he? At least there's no one around that I can see."

"He's probably waiting at the first truck stop or rest area," Duke snapped. "Now do as I say."

Good Lord, Leslie thought, just the idea of marriage had the man completely unhinged. He already thought he could order her around like a slave.

"I will not!" she cried.

"Leslie, the man packs a .357 Magnum in a shoulder holster, and God only knows what he plans to do with it. Now get in the sleeper!"

"No! I don't care if he's got a cannon mounted on his dashboard. I am sick and tired of being penned up back there. I'll take my chances, thank you. Besides, we've got a lot to talk about, and I refuse to do it over the intercom."

Duke was busy getting the huge diesel under way again, but he cast Leslie a burning glare.

"Have it your way, then," he said tightly, his jaw tense. Once back in the flow of traffic, he turned to look at Leslie briefly before snarling out a rapid series of questions. "How in hell did you get a message out?" he asked. "Or were you really working for Phillips after all, and they got worried when Callahan reported he hadn't seen you? What happened, did you get cold feet when you saw the long arm of the law reaching out to get me? Is that why you're not worried about Callahan now? Because he saw the police stop me and thinks I'm about to be hauled to jail?"

Leslie stared at Duke, openmouthed.

"You just never give up, do you? Well, you're way off again. I had an indelible marker up my sleeve when we stopped that first night in Pennsylvania, and I left a message on the wall of the booth. God only knows why it took so long for someone to respond to it. I expected you to be stopped the next morning."

Duke's jaw visibly relaxed, and he shrugged. "People don't want to get involved. Or maybe that telegram put them off for a while, but then they became suspicious when they didn't hear any more from you." He looked over at Leslie again, this time with a wry smile. "Sorry. I didn't mean to yell at you. I'm just a little unnerved by what happened back there. I suppose you think I should be more appreciative of your quick thinking. Or did you have that all planned out?"

"You know darned well I didn't," Leslie replied, only partly mollified by his slight apology. "I've been hoping I could get word to someone that I was really all right and that the message was a mistake, but I had no idea what I'd do or say if the police did stop you. I just had to play it by ear."

"Well, you've certainly got us in a mess now," Duke said, his mouth working as he chewed on his lower lip.

"A mess now!" Leslie stared at him in disbelief. Of all the ungrateful people she had ever met, Duke Caldwell had to take the prize. "There you were, turning red as a beet but acting as if you'd swallowed your tongue, while those patrolmen accused you of being a criminal abductor of women and me of being your—your immoral purpose! I had to do something! And you certainly don't need to worry about there being any wedding bells in our future. I'll get the story scuttled as soon as I can get to a telephone."

Leslie shuddered a little as she said that. For one brief moment back there, as Loren Barstow congratulated them, she had almost pictured herself standing at the altar with Duke at her side. But it was, after all, a ridiculous idea. He didn't love her, apparently couldn't love any woman. Didn't even want to try. She glanced over at that handsome, well-defined profile, the lock of black hair that perpetually tried to fall forward over his forehead now being subjected to a vigorous combing back with strong, tense fingers. What on earth was he so nervous about now? She had said she'd set the rumor straight as soon as possible. Then came a thunderbolt that made the heaven's mightiest efforts pale by comparison.

"No, you won't," Duke said. "We'll have to go through with it. But we can't wait until June. The political campaign will be in full swing by then, and I'll want you at my side from the beginning. I think we'd better plan the wedding for the first of April."

For a moment Leslie felt as if the world had come to a complete halt, her blood had stopped flowing and her heart had stopped beating. Duke's words bounced around in her head like an echo in a mountain valley.

"What?" she squeaked reflexively, although she knew perfectly well what he had said.

"I said—"

"I know, I heard you," Leslie interrupted as suddenly her brain and body came back to life with a rush that left her breathless. "That's...ridiculous. You don't want to get married. Why on earth would you suggest such a thing?"

Duke cast a quick glance her way. "You didn't say you don't want to. At least one of us should be pleased."

"I was talking about general principles!" Leslie cried. "You have made it perfectly clear to me that you don't believe in old-fashioned love and marriage at all, and that's the only kind of marriage I'd ever want. So why on earth would I be pleased to marry you? Forget it. I won't do it. And you still haven't answered my question. Why?"

"Several reasons," Duke replied grimly. "For one, I doubt if we could even get to a telephone before the news of our cozy little arrangement in this truck and our impending marriage starts spreading. If I know Loren, he'll buttonhole the first reporter he meets in Memphis and give him a little off-the-record scoop that will be on the record as soon as the reporter can get to a phone. We may not be as newsworthy as the president, but the elements of that story you gave those officers, together with your little message on the wall, will make damned good copy. If we stick with it, it will sound like the romance of the century. If we call it off, I'll look like a damned fool, and you'll be hounded by reporters day and night asking for the intimate details of your abduction. Phillips would have an even more effective story than if you'd actually been deliberately out to destroy me. I can't let everything I've worked so hard for go down the tubes for want of the courage to say a few words in front of a preacher. Besides—" he gave Leslie a wry smile "—Loren seemed to think we'd make a good pair."

"A lot he knows!" Leslie snapped. "He's been married four times. Why don't we just tell everyone the truth? Or doesn't that ever occur to you?"

Duke gave a short harsh laugh. "Who on earth would believe it? The story you gave those patrolmen was a hundred times simpler and more believable. Besides, it makes the kind of romantic copy the media will eat up."

So that was it. Duke was so concerned with his precious image that he'd even marry her to protect it. "I suppose I should be flattered that you want me for window dressing in your campaign," she said bitterly, "so that you can really look like the perfect candidate. Well, I'm sorry. The answer is still no. I'll just have to take my lumps from the press and let it go at that, and I'm afraid you'll have to, too. I can't see committing myself until death do us part for that, even if the entire Imperial Valley turns to salt."

Tight-lipped, she stared out the window, cursing the foolish tears that came to her eyes as she said no to marrying Duke Caldwell. If only he hadn't made it so clear that he felt marriage was a foolish, old-fashioned convention, she might even be tempted, despite her knowledge that he didn't love her. For one thing was becoming more and more obvious. She did love him. She would have laid her neck on the chopping block before she'd have let those patrolmen take him away believing he'd misused her in any way. What perverse fate, she wondered morosely, had decreed she would fall in love with Duke Caldwell?

"Uh, Leslie," Duke said tentatively, his voice taking on its soft, velvety edge, "I'm afraid I may have given you the wrong impression about my attitude toward marriage."

"Oh? I thought you were perfectly clear on it," Leslie replied tightly. What kind of tricky footwork was he about to try now? Not that it would make any difference. She could see some kind of trap being laid from a mile off.

"Well . . . while it's true that I've always planned on dodging the bullet myself, I've always felt strongly that marriage, once entered into, should be taken seriously. My father's experience taught me that. And I would make every effort to be a good husband and father for our children. This may sound very opportunistic after what I said before, but your little story back there made me do some quick revaluating, and I don't think the idea of our marriage is a bad one at all. We do get along well, especially considering the rocky start we had, and I think there's mutual respect between us. Certainly there's a mutual physical attraction. After all, that's not such a bad basis for a marriage, is it? People all over the world begin arranged marriages with far less than that to go on and make successful lives together. I know I don't have any kind of leverage to force you into it, and I wouldn't use it if I did. But I would appreciate it if you'd give the idea some serious thought." He looked over at Leslie and raised his eyebrows questioningly as he gave her his most appealing smile. "Will you at least do that?"

Leslie flicked a quick glance at him and licked her lips nervously. Her common sense told her that she should tell him in no uncertain terms that she would do no such thing. Only hours ago he had expressed his desire to "educate" her out of her old-fashioned ways. How could she believe that he would really be a loyal and devoted husband? How could she marry him, with only the hope that someday he might come to love her as she did him? But something stronger than her mind kept her silent, pushing forward a demon that would not be denied.

"I suppose I might think about it," she said reluctantly.

"Good. That's all that I ask." Duke's voice vibrated with relief. He reached over and squeezed Leslie's hand. "Maybe the best thing for me to do now is to court you like a proper gentleman."

"I don't think so," Leslie said, taking the large warm hand and returning it to the steering wheel. "If I'm going to think this over, I need to be left alone to do just that." And God knew that if he started "courting" her, she'd lose any ability she had to think straight. "The best thing for you to do now is to figure out how to get me on my way to St. Louis as soon as possible. If you're right about Loren leaking the story right away and about how eager the press will be to tell it, there's apt to be someone on our trail by tomorrow, and I'd just as soon not have my picture spread all over looking like this." She glanced down at her wrinkled slacks and jacket in disgust. "I need a place to buy some decent new clothes and get cleaned up before I go anywhere. Where are we now?" She looked out at the unfamiliar, hilly landscape, suddenly realizing that she had crossed over a thousand miles of the continent without seeing anything. "Are we still in Missouri?"

"Just barely," Duke replied. "We'll be in Arkansas in a few minutes." He paused and frowned. "I'd forgotten about your St. Louis job. I'd really like to take you on to California to meet my father and see my place. I think you'll like it." Seeing Leslie's scowl, he added quickly. "But I guess you could fly out as soon as you're through there."

"And I guess I can't," Leslie replied crossly. Did Duke now think he could run her life? "I have to get back to New York and take care of paying for my sister's car repairs so she and Ted don't have to take taxis all over town. And while you're making plans for me, you can forget about the first of April, even if I should go insane and decide to marry you. I have a job in El Salvador then, and I'll be there for at least two weeks, maybe longer, and I don't intend to drop that opportunity, either, just for your convenience."

Duke sighed heavily. "I guess I can cope with that. But why don't you let me loan you the money for the blasted car? It can't be that much, and I'll make it strictly business, the standard interest rates."

"Why not do the Fling promotion instead?" Leslie countered. "I'm sure the judges would pick you, and it would be a great joke on Cliveden Phillips."

"What makes you so sure I'd win?"

Leslie eyed Duke speculatively. Should she tell him? No, probably not. She smiled mysteriously instead. "I happen to have inside information on what they're looking for. My friend Susan Martin works for the agency in charge."

"I don't think it would work out," Duke said after a few moments of thought. "Clive would scotch the promotion before it hit the market. But it might be fun to tweak his nose by entering. I'll think about it . . . if meanwhile you'll let me help you out so you can come to California. Fair enough?"

"I suppose so," Leslie replied, wondering if she were now on some kind of roller coaster that she dared not get off. "Now, about St. Louis?" she reminded hopefully.

"Yes, well . . ." Duke rubbed his chin thoughtfully. "If there's no sign of Callahan when I get fueled up ahead, I'll stop at the first nice-looking motel and get a room so you can clean up. There should be a large enough town ahead to have some shops, too. We won't be anyplace that has an airfield until tomorrow when we get to Little Rock, but we should be there before noon. Okay?"

"Why can't we go on to Little Rock tonight?" Leslie asked quickly, the idea of spending another night in the truck now more disturbing than ever. "Or maybe I could just stay in the motel room tonight."

Duke grinned—a very self-satisfied grin, Leslie thought, as though he were well aware of why she was disturbed.

"As far as going on to Little Rock," he replied, "we can't because I can only legally drive ten hours out of twenty-four, and I'm pushing the limit now. However, the motel sounds like a good idea, for both of us. I'm not leaving you alone, as long as I don't know where our old friend Callahan has disappeared to. I now have a prospective bride to take care of, you know," he concluded with a reappearance of that mischievous wink. When Leslie made a sour face at him, he chuckled. "Come on, little love, you may as well smile at me. You can't look so grim and serious forever, even if you do have the world's weightiest decision to make. Frowning won't make it any easier."

He was right, Leslie thought as she did smile, at first reluctantly and then with a warmth that came unbidden in response to the soft glow in Duke's dark eyes. If she was going to make up her mind halfway intelligently, it would have to be on the basis of both the positive and negative aspects of Duke's proposal. The way she felt when he smiled at her like that was certainly positive.

CHAPTER EIGHT

A SHORT TIME LATER Duke stopped at a small-town service station that advertised both groceries and diesel fuel.

"No sign of Callahan, and there's a dress shop across the street that's still open if you hurry," Duke reported a short time later, poking his head into the sleeper where he had insisted Leslie retreat until he was sure that they were free of Mr. Callahan's presence. "I'll inquire about places that we might stay, while you shop."

"Hallelujah!" Leslie cried. "Free at last."

Duke had given her the key to the padlock so that she could retrieve her camera bag and the billfold within it, and she now grabbed the billfold and hastened out of the truck and headed for the little shop that Duke pointed out to her. Soon she returned with a large box containing not only some blue jeans and fresh blouses and sweaters, which she usually wore for her work, but two pretty spring dresses and a pair of simple pumps. She needed them since she hadn't packed for St. Louis at all, she excused herself, ignoring the fact that she had immediately thought upon seeing the dresses that Duke had never seen her wearing anything really attractive.

"It looks as though you bought the place out," Duke commented, giving Leslie's large package a raised eyebrow inspection.

"A typically male remark," Leslie retorted. "I do need some things for my trip to St. Louis, you know. Did you have any luck on a place to stay?"

"I believe so. There's an inn overlooking the Mississippi River not far from here that's supposed to be very nice, and they even have a dance band on Saturday night. I thought you might enjoy something like that after being cooped up for so long."

And here goes the courtship part, Leslie thought wryly, but she smiled anyway. "It sounds very nice. I am used to a much more active life than I've had lately."

"Good. I've made reservations for us already, and I even talked the owner of this service station into renting me his car so we can leave the truck behind for the night. Are you ready to go?"

"As soon as I get my camera bag," Leslie replied.

"It will be safe here, I'm sure," Duke said. "Or do you feel more secure when your cameras are with you?"

"I do indeed," Leslie nodded, surprised at Duke's understanding. "I worked so long to be able to afford the best I like to know exactly where they are at all times."

"It really feels like spring here," Duke commented a few minutes later as they drove along a winding road, the windows of the car open to the balmy air.

"Mmm-hmm," Leslie agreed, "and the trees are so much further along with their new leaves than the ones were in New York. This is really beautiful." She gestured to the carpet of wildflowers beneath the tall oak and hickory trees along the roadside. She was trying valiantly to look at her surroundings with her photographer's eye, as she usually did, instead of devoting far too much attention to the handsome man beside her.

She wanted to draw back, to try to be objective about him. But when he spoke, she found her eyes drawn to him, to the strong jaw below the sensitive mouth, to the not-quite-straight nose with its well-defined bridge beneath those sweeping black brows. There was such a solid strength to the way his neck was set squarely on wide, muscular shoulders, a touch of grace, too, in the proud way he held himself erect. This was not, she decided, a man who would ever slouch or grovel. He seemed born to lead. Was she born to follow?

Duke caught Leslie studying him and gave her a winning smile.

"Trying to decide if you could stand looking at me for the next fifty years?" he asked teasingly.

Leslie felt her cheeks grown warm, but she replied tartly, "No, I've already decided about that. I couldn't possibly. But perhaps with the help of plastic surgery—" She giggled as Duke reached over and gave her nose a tweak.

"You are determined that I'm vain about my appearance, aren't you?" he demanded, giving Leslie a critical look. "Why?"

She shrugged. "You do look startlingly like a certain famous personage," she replied.

"So? That doesn't make lemons grow any better. And it's not something I can take any credit for."

That was interesting, Leslie thought. It was almost as if he didn't like the way he looked. However, she doubted it was a real burden to him. "I can't believe you're that blasé about it," she said.

"I've had to learn to be," he replied, giving Leslie a sideways look. "Believe it or not, I'd rather look distinctively like just myself instead of someone else. I used to pick fights in school, hoping someone would mash my nose or break my jaw or otherwise rearrange my features. You, for instance, may think you'd like to look like Katharine Hepburn or Jackie O, but I assure you, I like you looking exactly like Leslie Lyon and no one else."

"I never thought about it that way," Leslie said, frowning as she meditated on Duke's complaint. Strange. So many people worked overtime trying to imitate someone they admired. Duke only wanted to be an original. That was definitely something in his favor. She turned to study his face again, trying to analyze what features were uniquely his, for she knew she could never truly mistake him for anyone else.

"Well?" Duke asked gruffly as she continued to stare at him.

"Oh, sorry!" Leslie laughed. "I've found that each person has some feature or part of his face that seems essential to capturing his character, so I was trying to figure out how best to photograph you in order to bring out what I consider to be the real, unique Duke Caldwell. Force of habit. You'd have to get used to that. I do it all the time, even with total strangers. I seldom forget a face."

Duke chuckled. "Not a lethal flaw in your character." Then he laughed outright and, at Leslie's questioning look, said, "I have a feeling that this is going to be one of the strangest approaches to a potential marriage in modern history. If it works out, we ought to write one of those 'how-to' books."

"That's a mighty big if," Leslie retorted. "I'm a very long way from making a decision." She tried to ignore the knowing smile that Duke gave her. He really had no reason to think she was inclined in his favor at all, except for the fact that he knew she was attracted to him physically. Maybe he thought he could parlay that into a yes in a moment of weakness. Well, she wasn't going to let that happen. There was too much at stake.

"This must be the place," Duke said, slowing the car as they approached a large, hand-carved sign that said Braemer's Seven Hickory Inn. He turned down a lane between rows of neatly trimmed yews and stopped before a large two-story building of rustic design with a wide veranda decorated with rows of small, festive lights along the roof and railing. Beds of bright red and yellow tulips framed the staircase. "Looks like a pleasant place to pretend being Mr. and Mrs. Caldwell for a night."

"Mr. and Mrs. Caldwell?" Leslie cried. "You didn't—" She stared at Duke, wide-eyed. "I thought we'd have separate rooms! You should have asked me—"

"For God's sake, don't panic," Duke scolded. "If you could trust me in that sleeping bag, you can certainly trust me in a king-sized bed. And it seemed only practical to me that, if you're going to make a sensible decision on whether you want to spend your life with me, you should get to know me as well as time permits. It's damned hard to get to know someone sleeping in the next room."

"I can't see how being with you when you're asleep is going to help any," Leslie snapped, "unless you talk in your sleep. And so far I haven't noticed that you do." It was becoming obvious that she had guessed right about his plan to weaken her defenses. "Besides, things are different now. I'm not sure I do trust you."

"And that's exactly why you should," Duke snarled back, a dark frown drawing his brows together. "I'm a hell of a lot more interested in making a good impres-

sion on you now than I was last night. I know damn well
I could have seduced you when you and I were all
snuggled up after your nightmare, but I didn't. Instead, I lay awake half the night wondering why I
hadn't! As a result, after we've had dinner and done a
few turns on the dance floor, I'm going to be too tired
to do anything but sleep for a good eight hours. So
don't spend any extra time worrying about your precious virginity being in danger tonight!''

"You needn't yell at me. It's not my fault we're in this
predicament," Leslie said, returning Duke's glare.

"I'll yell if I damn well please! I'm tired and hungry
and need a shower, and I'm not in the mood to cater to
your delicate sensibilities. You may not think it's your
fault, but my life was sure one hell of a lot simpler before I met you. So you can consider it part of your education that I sometimes get tired and cross and
unreasonable, and I have absolutely no intention of
apologizing for it. Now are you ready to go in or aren't
you?"

Duke's sudden flare-up had taken Leslie by surprise,
but as he roared on, a pleasantly warm feeling replaced
her earlier anxiety. There was something so comfortingly normal about his response. Her own father was
given to ranting like that when he was tired and things
weren't going the way he wanted them to. And she had
learned from watching her mother that the best way to
deal with it was to let it pass and not rant back.

"Sure," she replied with a smile.

For a moment Duke looked surprised, then he returned Leslie's smile with a little shake of his head before he opened his door and came around to help Leslie
out.

"They're going to think we're a couple of the tacki-est-looking customers they've ever had," Leslie com-mented softly as they mounted the steps together.

"Wait until they see us at dinner," Duke replied. "Even I have some more decent clothes to put on."

While Duke signed the guest register, Leslie surveyed the huge lobby area, admiring some excellent wildlife photographs on the walls identified as the work of C. F. Braemer. Then she wandered over to gaze out the wall of windows and glass doors at the back, which opened onto a huge deck overlooking a steep wooded slope. Below, catching the last rays of sunlight, was the mighty Mississippi, a barge tow in the center pushing its long train of cargo downstream toward the Gulf of Mexico.

"Look," she said, pointing as Duke came up beside her. "What do you suppose it's carrying?"

"Probably grain," Duke replied. "Trucks take it to the river ports, and then it's loaded on barges."

"Did you ever think you'd like to captain a river tug instead of driving your truck?" Leslie asked as she and Duke followed a round little woman dressed in a homespun peasant costume to the curving staircase that led up from the lobby to a balcony along one side.

"What boy who's read Mark Twain hasn't?" Duke replied.

The woman flung open the door to a spacious room, done in the same rustic, beautiful decor as the lobby.

"We're serving cocktails in the bar now," she said in a soft, slightly accented voice. "Dinner begins at six, and there will be a polka band starting at eight. If you need anything, just call me."

"A polka band?" Leslie asked.

The woman nodded.

"I love to polka," Leslie said happily. Then she looked at Duke's tired face. "But you're probably too tired for that," she said sympathetically.

"I'll gather my strength somehow," he said with a grin for both Leslie and the young woman, who had looked at him anxiously.

"Good. It is fun," she said before leaving them with a pleasant smile.

"This is charming," Leslie said, looking around the room with its bright red and beige homespun drapes framing a sliding door, which opened onto a balcony that overlooked the same scene Leslie had admired from the lobby. Covering the huge bed was a beautiful hand worked quilt. There were braided rugs on the polished floor and dark pine furnishings, which all looked as if they had been handcrafted by meticulous craftsmen. She tossed her box of new clothing on the bed and set her camera bag carefully on the low dresser beside it. "Why don't you take a little nap while I get cleaned up?" she suggested to Duke, who was still standing near the door, watching her. "Or would you rather shower first?" When he did not reply, she cocked her head and asked, "Is something wrong?"

"No." Duke came toward her, a bemused smile quirking one corner of his mouth. "I was just wondering if you're the most amazing woman I've ever met or if I'm just losing my mind." He sank down to the edge of the bed with a tired sigh and looked up at her.

"I think you're just worn out," Leslie replied. "Hallucinating. I'm not amazing at all." She moved her box of clothing to a chair. "Lie down and shut your eyes. I'll wake you when I'm through."

Duke nodded, and before Leslie had time to gather all of her things together to take into the bath, he was asleep. She looked at him, his face relaxed, the tired lines less harsh, his mouth softly curved up at the corners. It was, indeed, a pleasant face to look at. One she would never tire of. He had already called her fascinating and amazing. That was a beginning, wasn't it? Or did those words come easily to him? Were they only words he knew a woman would like to hear?

Leslie took her time with a hot bath, which helped relax her body, tense from the strange events of the past few days and hours, and a hot shower afterward to give her hair a thorough scrubbing. She brushed her hair until it shone in silky abandon about her small, piquant face, then applied a touch of eye shadow, some blusher and lipstick from the small kit she always carried in her camera bag. Wrinkling her nose in distaste at the long cut above her left elbow, she managed to apply a fresh bandage and then put on the pale green dress she had just purchased. With its elbow-length puffed sleeves and full skirt, it was ideal for dancing a polka, she thought, pleased with the image she saw in the mirror. She tiptoed back into the main room and looked at her watch. It was almost six-thirty. She should wake Duke, but he looked so comfortable.... With a small sigh Leslie tore her eyes away from him and walked softly over to the window. Just looking at him made her ache in such confusing ways. One of the aches was from wanting him in a way she had never wanted a man before. The ache she knew she could assuage at almost any time by simply giving Duke the cues that said she was willing to make love. The other was deeper and darker, an empty longing to have him love her, not to have him say he'd be a loyal husband because that was the right thing to do but because she was the only woman he wanted for his wife. Until something made that ache go away, she could never agree to marry him, and what, besides a change of heart on Duke's part, might make that happen? She had no idea.

"Turn around. The back looks terrific."

Startled at the sudden sound of his deep, husky voice, Leslie whirled, her wide skirt flying.

"Very, very pretty," Duke said, leaning on one elbow and rubbing his eyes sleepily. "I'd say you're a cinch to be the prettiest polka-er in the place."

"Thank you, sir," Leslie replied, making a deep curtsy, "but I'm afraid you flatter me. However, I will admit to being the hungriest."

"Oh, no, I claim that title," Duke said, pushing himself off the bed and stretching luxuriously. He picked up the small suitcase he had brought from the truck. "I'll be with you in record time," he promised, retreating to the bath.

While Leslie waited, she gave a few moments' thought to calling New York to let Susan or Melody know she was all right but quickly rejected the idea. Anything she might tell them would only lead to more questions than she could possibly answer in one telephone call. She was often gone, and Duke's telegram probably hadn't caused them concern at all. She would call from St. Louis.

If Duke dressed in casual truckers' garb had been outstanding, he was positively smashing in dark blue slacks and a lighter blue sports coat worn over a cream-colored cotton cable-knit sweater. Leslie was sure that every woman in the spacious dining room stopped chewing and gawked at him for several minutes as they were led to their table by a waiter dressed in lederhosen. It would be hard, she thought, for even a secure wife to cope with having a husband who inspired that

kind of attention from other women. For one who knew
she had been chosen only out of desperation, it would
be intolerable. Added to her other misgivings, that
thought put a real damper on the enthusiasm Leslie had
felt for an evening of relatively harmless pleasure—if
any time she spent with Duke Caldwell could now be
called harmless.

Duke, however, seemed not to notice her sudden silence as he ordered huge, frosty mugs of beer for them
to enjoy while they waited for their dinner.

"Shall we drink to our future?" he suggested, raising his glass and giving her a warm, intimate smile.

"No," Leslie said shortly, feeling suddenly as if a trap
were closing on her. She gazed at Duke across the pool
of amber liquid in her own glass. "Let's just drink to
the future. May it be kind to both of us."

"I can't argue with that," Duke agreed, touching his
glass to hers before taking a deep draft. "You've been
very quiet since we sat down. What's wrong?" he asked
softly.

Leslie shook her head, staring into her glass. She was
not especially fond of beer, she thought, but maybe with
enough beer and wine, she would be able to enjoy the
evening. As for telling Duke what was wrong...

"It's nothing in particular. I just keep seeing more
and more problems."

"Then look at me instead," Duke ordered, lifting
Leslie's chin with his hand and tracking her eyes with his
so that she could not look away, a trick that she found
disconcerting. "Do I look like a problem? And if so,
why? I'm honest, hardworking and, in case it interests
you, very rich. I have my own teeth and hair, good
health, reasonable intelligence—although you may

doubt that. I can even do the polka. What more could any woman ask for?''

Leslie finally succeeded in looking away without creating a scene. She wanted to scream ''That's not the point!'' but managed to control herself, instead asking tightly, ''Can we talk about something else? What do you suppose became of Mr. Callahan? Did the sight of those patrolmen scare him off?''

''That's the only explanation I can think of,'' Duke agreed. ''Although we may still not be rid of him. He may have had some particular spot he wanted to get to today, and he's waiting there, knowing I'll go by eventually.''

''Isn't there some other route we could take to Little Rock in the morning? I don't really relish the thought of having that man back on our trail, especially since you told me about his gun. I'm beginning to wonder if there isn't some other reason he's following your truck. What are you carrying in the trailer?''

''Veterinary pharmaceuticals. Antibiotics that have to be kept refrigerated. I've thought about that, wondering if he might have some idea of stealing some and selling them to the ranchers between here and home, but I doubt it. It really wouldn't be worth the risk.''

Leslie shrugged. ''Maybe he isn't smart enough to figure that out,'' she suggested.

''I wish I thought that were true,'' Duke said with a frown as his eyes scanned Leslie's face soberly. ''I don't like feeling that you're in danger, and I'm not going to rest until I find out exactly what Callahan's reason for following us has been.''

''I appreciate that,'' Leslie said, forcing herself to smile at Duke in spite of the flush of confusion she felt. When he looked at her like that and gave the smallest indication of caring, she felt like hurling herself into his arms. *I'm going to drive myself crazy yet,* she thought, taking another long drink of her beer. She looked up in relief as the waiter appeared by her side. "Oh, good, here's dinner," she said, trying to smile more brightly. "At least I'll no longer be in danger of starving."

Leslie loved German food, and between the delicious jaeger schnitzel and an excellent wine, she was soon in an almost carefree state of mind, giggling delightedly at Duke's stories of life in the lemon groves. The band appeared, dressed in authentic German costumes, and as soon as they struck up the first polka, a young couple, also costumed, took the floor, apparently to break the ice for the rest of the customers. They were both apple-cheeked and blond, the girl with her hair in a coronet of braids on top of her head.

"They're good!" Leslie exclaimed, reaching for the decanter of wine. She frowned as Duke took it from her hand. "Stop that! I want another glass."

Duke shook his head. "Enough. I don't want to have to pick you up off the dance floor. Come on, let's show them they're not the only polka-ers in town." He stood up and took off his jacket, then held his hand out to Leslie, who was still frowning, not at all sure she wanted to dance with someone so bossy. It wasn't as if she were drunk, for heaven's sake! But then, it was probably best if she didn't have any more wine. It was quite warm in the room already and would be even warmer once they began to move. Giving Duke a reproving look, she extended her hand.

"All right, Mr. Party Pooper," she said. "Let's see how good you are."

It was not many whirls around the floor later before Leslie was very glad she'd had no more wine. Duke was terrific, but he kept up a pace that would have made the soberest dancer dizzy.

"Where did you learn to polka like this?" Leslie said with a gasp, having to shout to make herself heard above the band and the noise of the increasing crowd of dancers.

"Munich. How about you?"

"Milwaukee!" Leslie laughed. "But I've been to Bavaria, too. Isn't it lovely?"

Duke nodded and pulled Leslie against him as another couple collided briefly and then backed off with a quick, "Sorry folks!" On and on they danced, through at least half a dozen polkas.

"Let's take a break," Leslie finally said breathlessly at the end of one song. "I'm afraid I'm out of condition for a marathon."

"Good idea," Duke agreed, taking out his handkerchief and mopping his brow as they returned to their table. "I'd forgotten how very active a polka can be."

He was just helping Leslie into her chair when the young woman in the German costume who had started the polka dancing came up to them.

"I'm Maria Braemer. Would you mind if I borrowed your husband for a few dances?" she asked Leslie but only gave her a brief glance as her eyes went to Duke's face. "He is such a fine dancer. That was my brother Carl I danced with earlier. The other boys don't ask me because they are afraid they aren't good enough."

"Go right ahead," Leslie replied, although it was obvious her permission was not really required. Duke had already taken the woman's arm with an "I'd be delighted," and started ushering her back toward the floor. "Humph. Quick recovery," Leslie muttered. But then, she probably shouldn't have been surprised. Leopards didn't change their spots, and Maria was quite pretty, not to mention that her low-cut peasant blouse revealed a lot of bouncy bosom.

As Duke and Maria danced on energetically, Leslie became increasingly peeved. *Come on, now,* she told herself, *you have no reason to be jealous. He's not really your husband.* And, she thought grimly, as he started still another dance, he certainly wouldn't be if he kept this up. She was thirsty. The table had been cleared, and she planned to wait until Duke returned to order another beer, but if he was going to spend all night on the dance floor with that blond floozy, she was going to go ahead. She signaled the waiter and ordered two more steins of beer. Instead of the waiter returning with the order, it was the dancing blonde's brother who brought it. He beamed at Leslie as he set the beer steins on the table with a flourish.

"Would you do me the honor of a dance?" he asked. "I have a break from my duties at the bar, and I see that my sister has cornered your husband."

"I'd love to!" Leslie quickly took a long drink of her beer, then got to her feet. "Lead on!"

Young Carl was an excellent dancer, smaller and even somewhat quicker than Duke. Leslie threw herself into the dance with abandon, waving gaily to Duke as they whirled by. He did not seem to see her, his gaze somewhat glassy as he concentrated on Maria's cleavage. So much for loyalty and devotion, Leslie thought bitterly. He can't even pretend for one night. She turned a determined smile to Carl as the dance ended.

"Let's do that again! That was fun," she said. For several dances she concentrated on Carl, not wanting to give Duke the satisfaction of thinking she was keeping track of him. When she finally did look around, he was nowhere in sight, either on the dance floor or at their table. But his jacket was gone. Nor was Maria anywhere to be seen. Leslie felt a numbing chill go through her. He wouldn't! Not if he'd meant what he said about wanting to make a good impression on her so that she'd agree to marry him. But maybe he was one of those men who just couldn't pass up an opportunity. Well, it was a good thing she'd found that out!

The dance couldn't end soon enough for Leslie. She thanked Carl and murmured something about having to turn in for an early start in the morning, then returned to their table only long enough to grab her purse and notice that Duke hadn't touched the beer she'd ordered for him. My goodness, but he'd been in a hurry to leave! Did he really think she wouldn't notice that he was missing? Trembling from head to foot with a combination of rage and something she did not identify, she tore up the stairs and paused outside the door to their room. *I'll just pack up and leave right now,* she resolved as she inserted her key into the lock. The sound of a female voice made her pause.

"Stop that!" the voice cried in high-pitched tones, then giggled. "Oh, you are such a bad boy."

"Oh, for God's sake," Leslie muttered to herself. "This is the last straw. I am going to give that egotistical woman-chasing Romeo a piece of my mind!" With that she turned the key and flung open the door with such force that it hit the wall with a loud bang.

The room was dark except for the flickering light from the television screen, whereon a nubile young actress was engaged in a passionate grapple with an overmuscled hunk. Duke was in bed, asleep, all alone, the covers drawn up beneath his bare arms and shoulders.

"Oh, my," Leslie whispered, feeling weak and slightly sick to her stomach at the letdown. She had certainly been way off base. Or had she? Had Maria already left, after putting Duke in a pleasantly relaxed mood? Quietly she closed the door and then started to tiptoe into the room.

"You don't have to sneak," Duke's voice growled huskily. "Your grand entrance woke me."

"I'm sorry. I didn't know you were asleep," Leslie said, glancing briefly in Duke's direction. "I thought you'd still be up."

"I know exactly what you thought," Duke retorted. "You thought you'd find me and little Maria in bed. Disappointed?"

"I thought no such thing," Leslie denied hotly. "Although I certainly did wonder why you danced with her as if someone had handed you the Red Shoes and why you disappeared at the same time as she did."

"She wouldn't quit, so I finally told her I was tired. I saw you were having a good time, so I didn't bother to drag you off with me. On the way out I met her mother, who happens to be one of the owners of this place. She scolded Maria for wearing an old man out and sent her back to work at the bar. End of story."

"Oh, so your luck ran out when Mama appeared," Leslie snapped, squirming as she tried to undo the back zipper on her dress. "Too bad. Better luck next time."

"There wasn't going to be any this time, and there won't be any next time. I found out what I wanted to know. Now get over and let me help you before you tear your dress." He snapped on the light by the bed and sat up, revealing that he was naked at least to the waist.

"Darn thing's caught," Leslie muttered. She glanced apprehensively at Duke. "Don't you have anything on?"

"Pajama bottoms," he replied. "See?" He threw back the covers and revealed that he was, indeed, wearing dark brown pajamas. "Now come on and sit down here." He patted the side of the bed.

Leslie moved reluctantly toward him and did as he had told her.

"What did you mean that you found out what you wanted to know?" she asked, the nape of her neck tingling as Duke fussed with her zipper.

"I mean I thought it was the perfect opportunity to find out if you'd be jealous. If you weren't, I figured there wouldn't be much chance of your agreeing to marry me. As it is, you're in as fine a snit as I've seen. Good omen."

"I am not in a snit!" Leslie retorted, trying to squelch the honest little voice that told her that that was as big a lie as she'd ever told. "I just thought your behavior was—extremely inappropriate for someone who was pretending to be married."

"How about yours, out there with Maria's brother trying to get even? I saw the way you were looking before you started to dance. Madder than hell, I'd say."

"I was not. I was only wondering if your eyeballs were going to fall out and slide down Maria's cleavage. Ooooh!"

"There we go." Duke had freed the zipper and then run a tantalizing finger down Leslie's spine.

"Stop that!" Leslie cried as he also unfastened her bra and began to push both dress and bra down from her shoulders.

"Huh-uh," Duke replied, tucking a strong arm around Leslie inside her dress and just beneath her breasts. He nuzzled her shoulder and then pressed his cheek against it. "Ah, such lovely, silky skin." As Leslie wriggled, trying to fight against the seductive warmth of first Duke's lips and then his cheek, he went on, "I'm not letting you go until you give up that nonsense about Maria. I can tell you're still upset. What do you think I did, invite her up here for a quickie?"

"For all I know, you may have," Leslie replied tightly. "She looked willing enough, and you're clever enough to have made up the rest of it." She drew her breath in sharply as Duke's hand slid beneath her unfastened bra and softly caressed her breast at the same time as he continued to nuzzle and caress her back. Waves of warmth washed over her like a soft fog. *Get up and move,* she told herself, *before it's too late,* but none of her movable parts responded.

"I can prove quite conclusively that I didn't," Duke murmured in her ear.

"H-how?" Leslie asked, twisting her head back to try to look at him. The deep, burning glow that she saw in his eyes held her there, fascinated, and she turned in his arms without protest as he pulled her around toward him. Then he took her hand and placed it firmly over the hard evidence of his desire and held it there.

"I'm not seventeen anymore, you know," he said softly, brushing his lips against hers.

The sensations that communicated themselves to Leslie were like nothing she had ever experienced before. She felt light-headed but powerful, almost omnipotent. It was like the rush she had read about happening from some drugs. Her lips parted and swollen-feeling, she stared wide-eyed at this man who could

so magically change the way she felt. This was more
than sensual desire—it was love, so deep and powerful
that it could instantly transform the way the whole
world seemed. Duke moved her hand away and placed
it on his thigh, and she absently stroked it, feeling the
steely muscle beneath the silky fabric.

"You've never felt that before?" Duke asked gently.

Leslie gave a small shake of her head. "Only some
groping in the dark back in high school," she said. "It
wasn't the same."

Duke smiled. "That's more like puppies playing, although it can get those puppies into a lot of trouble. The
real desire of a man for a woman is something much
deeper and stronger, something you should know
about. It can be very important to a marriage. To some
people it isn't, but I would never have suggested we
marry, in spite of the consequences, if you hadn't had
the damnedest talent for putting me in this condition,
even when I don't want to be."

"Why don't you want to be?" Leslie asked hoarsely.
Her dress and bra had slid down, and there was nothing she wanted more now than to press herself against
Duke's hard chest and feel the sensation of his softly
curling hair against her throbbing nipples.

"Because," Duke said, brushing Leslie's hair back
from her flushed face with tender strokes, "as even you
must be sophisticated enough to know, it is hell to get
this way and then have to turn it off. Which I shall have
to do—" he brushed his lips against Leslie's "—unless
you've changed your mind." His mouth found hers
again, moist and warm and full of promise. "I know
you want me, too," he said huskily, pulling her against
him with devastating effect. "It would be very lovely,
for both of us."

So lovely. Leslie's head whirled dizzily, her arms around Duke's broad back, every sense glorying in his nearness, the ache to have him teach her of that loveliness pounding like surf upon the shore. She felt overwhelmed by love for this man, who would release her even now if she but said the word. The long-unawakened woman in her cried out that, if ever anyone was to claim her body, he should be the one. He already had her heart. Marriage to him might come quite soon, and then again it might not, but whatever happened, there would never be anyone in her life quite like Duke Caldwell.

Leslie raised her head from where it lay nestled against the base of Duke's throat. She looked deep into those dark, long-lashed eyes and felt warm and secure. Deliberately she took his head between her hands and pulled it toward her until their lips were touching in a kiss that began as softly as a whisper and grew into a deafening roar of passionate interchange. With a deep groan of pleasure that shook Leslie to her very soul, Duke pulled her down as he lay back, cradling her against his shoulder and stroking her clothing downward and away, until she lay soft and warm against the contrasting hard rough warmth of his chest and the cool silkiness of his pajama bottoms.

"Your turn," Duke murmured, at the same time using his hands to caress and tease her skin, grown so sensitive that every touch was like fuel to the fire that burned ever higher within her. Emboldened by her own building desire, Leslie unfastened the tie of his pajama bottoms, pulling herself free so that she could remove them. She began some caressing of her own, at first tentative and then more daring until Duke gave a deep, sighing moan. She stopped and glanced at him questioningly.

"Don't stop, you're doing fine," he said softly, his eyes half closed. "I was just expressing my appreciation."

Leslie gave him a warm smile, a great wave of love filling her at his understanding. Impulsively, she flung herself upon him and kissed him, then pulled her head back and looked down at him "I'm afraid I got carried away," she said with a little laugh, "and now I'm in the wrong place. You'll have to teach me the rules."

"Your instincts are doing beautifully," Duke replied, his arms closing about her. "Rules are for people who don't have instincts." With one hand in her hair, he pressed her head toward him until their lips met again, while with the other he held her tightly against him, his movements leaving no doubt about his ever-increasing desire. The longing within Leslie grew so strong that she groaned rapturously at its intensity, even as she wondered how much stronger it could grow and how much longer she could wait for the final fulfillment of this promise of ecstasy beyond her wildest dreams.

As if he understood perfectly, Duke rolled onto his side with Leslie still in his embrace and took charge. Gentle lips explored peaks and valleys, sending wild currents of excitement surging through her. Completely lost in a vast panoply of sensations, Leslie retaliated with fingers that seemed as sensitive as rose petals, her ears finely tuned to the sounds of pleasure that told her Duke's arousal was as great as her own. It could not go on, there could be no more, she thought in wonder. Suddenly, just as she was sure she could bear it no longer, the feather-light touches stopped.

"Go on!" she cried hoarsely. "Don't stop!"

Triumphantly Duke rose above her, his eyes shining as he took possession of her, at first very gently and then with increasing strength until somewhere, above the earth, there came a new explosion made of heart and mind and muscle, soaring past the limits and then settling back in shuddering waves to rest upon a sunlit shore.

Silently Leslie stared at the man who lay quiet now upon her. Lovely? Tears trickled softly from the corners of her eyes. Lovely was such a feeble word for what she had felt. Heavenly? Perfect bliss? Ecstasy? None of them was adequate. She was so glad, so very glad, that she had experienced it. But, she thought suddenly, this did not have to be the end. It could go on and on for the rest of her life, with this man she loved!

"Duke," she said softly. "Duke, can you hear me?"

Duke opened his eyes sleepily. "Sorry," he mumbled, rolling to one side. "Didn't mean to squash you."

"No, that's not it," Leslie cried, turning toward him and caressing his cheek. "Listen to me. I'll marry you."

Duke's eyes opened wider and he frowned, raising his head from the pillow for a moment and shaking it.

"No, no, no," he said in a sleepily gruff voice. "Not now."

Leslie stared at Duke in confusion. Then she felt a sharp pang of anxiety. "Did I do something wrong?"

"Good Lord, no." Duke's eyes were closed again.

"Then what's changed? Don't you want me to marry you now?"

Duke sighed and opened one eye a small slit.

"Of course I do." His eye closed again.

Leslie leaned on one elbow and stared down at Duke. She would have sworn that all he wanted was a simple

yes for any reason at all. If he wasn't the most aggra-
vating man on earth, he was certainly in the running for
the title. First he held her prisoner like a criminal, then
he wanted to have an affair with her, then he ordered
her to marry him. If she'd agreed then, like some silly
sheep, he certainly wouldn't have argued. But now that
she'd said yes, he said no, not now. Why? She flopped
back down on the pillow with a thud.

"Sometimes I think you were put on this earth just to
drive me crazy," she said crossly. "I don't understand
what you want."

Duke's eyes flew open, and two strong arms suddenly scooped Leslie up and turned her over so that her
back was snuggled against his chest, spoon fashion.

"And sometimes I think you were put on this earth
just to keep me from sleeping!" he growled. "I seduced you! You'd marry the devil himself right now.
Now shut your eyes—and your mouth. We'll talk about
it in the morning!" He tightened his arms around her
soft, pliant body. "Good night, Leslie," he murmured
in her nape.

Leslie lay quietly, feeling Duke's grip on her relax as
he quickly drifted off to sleep again, her mind trying to
take in the implications of what Duke had said and
quickly coming to the realization that she had been very
wrong about one thing. She had been sure he would use
his power to arouse her, to convince her to marry him.
And now that she was convinced, he would not accept
her acquiescence. He was right, of course, although it
was a bit of an exaggeration to say that she'd even
marry the devil. She was quite sure she would say yes
again soon, when she was in full possession of her fa-
culties. But right now she did not want to come back to
earth completely. It felt so warm and good to be locked

in the arms of this remarkable man. How wonderful it would be to stay here forever and let the real world go on about its business somewhere far away. She tightened her arms around his as they held her, and he mumbled something in his sleep. Poor darling, he was so tired.

"Good night, Duke," Leslie whispered. "Sweet dreams."

CHAPTER NINE

THE JANGLING of the bedside telephone awakened Leslie to the real world again with a start. For a moment disoriented, she blinked and looked around her. It was early, the sun sending shadowy flickers through the trees along the riverbank. The phone rang again, and Duke, sprawled on his stomach, groaned. Who could it be this early? Leslie wondered as she turned to reach for the receiver.

"Hello?" she said huskily.

"Mrs. Caldwell?"

"Uh . . . yes," she replied, feeling strange at answering to that name.

"I'm sorry to disturb you so early. This is Bob Meyers at the service station. Someone broke into the cab of your truck last night. I've already called for a locksmith to repair the damage, and I've got the police on the way, but we'll need you people here as soon as possible to see what's missing."

"Oh, my!" Leslie gasped. "Th-thank you for calling. We'll be there as quickly as we can."

"What's wrong?" Duke asked, raising his head and blinking sleepily at Leslie.

"Someone broke into the truck cab during the night," she replied. "We've got to get there and talk to the police right away."

Duke sat up, instantly alert.

"Callahan," he said.

"Do you really think so?" Leslie felt a shudder of apprehension. What was that terrible man after?

"I'd bet on it," Duke replied, already on his way to the shower.

Darn! Leslie thought crossly as she watched his tall, naked body vanish into the bath. She was not eager to get back to reality again. In her dreams they had been lying in a huge round bed in a room like a Grecian pavilion, snuggling and talking and making love while an endless golden sun shone around them. But already Duke was concentrated on some of the less pleasant aspects of everyday reality—thievery and the man named Callahan, whose shadowy presence seemed to dog her footsteps like an evil spirit. She'd be lucky if Duke even remembered about last night.

She got out of bed and found a suitable outfit of new jeans, a bright red-and-white striped cotton blouse and a dark blue cardigan. Might as well wear the colors of a patriot ready to do battle, she thought grimly as she impatiently waited her turn at the bath.

"I'll come back for you as soon as I check things over," Duke announced as he came out of the bath, fully dressed but still toweling his hair vigorously.

"Come back for me? You will not!" Leslie cried. "I'll be with you in ten minutes. Don't you dare leave without me."

"Leslie," Duke said, placing his hands on her bare shoulders, "I want you to stay here. Callahan may be watching for us to come back. I'm beginning to think the man's really deranged. Please?" he added as Leslie glared at him.

"Duke—" Leslie mimicked his sober expression, placing her hands similarly on his shoulders. "I am coming with you. If you're still thinking of marrying me, you'd better plan on having a partner through thick and thin, not someone who comes when you whistle. Besides, the police will be there, and I doubt if Mr. Callahan or any other thieves will be hanging around.'' She watched as Duke's expression went from severe, to quizzical, to amused, as he looked down her naked body and back to her face.

"All right, but if I tell you to duck, do it," he said, then grinned. "Are you aware that you're standing there stark naked, and what that's doing to me?" He let his hands slide downward from her shoulders. "Have you no modesty left?"

Leslie flushed and stepped back quickly but lifted her chin and retorted, "It's a little late for that, isn't it?" Then she grabbed her pile of clothing and scurried in to take her shower.

As soon as they arrived at the service station, Bob Meyers came hurrying up to Duke, apologizing profusely.

"We don't have much crime around here," he said. "I can't imagine who'd have done this in the middle of the night and all. We're open till midnight and back at five in the morning, so they must have been here while we were gone."

Leslie had quickly gotten into the truck, and before Duke had even finished some preliminary words with the local police officer, she poked her head back out of the truck and called to him.

"What is it?" he asked.

"It's strange," she replied. "Things are messed up a little, but nothing seems to be missing."

A few minutes later Duke confirmed Leslie's findings.

"I guess there's nothing to report," he said to the police officer, and then, in an undertone to Leslie, "It looks like it must have been Callahan. There's something specific he thinks I've got that he was looking for. He didn't even take your pink bunny suit, so it can't be evidence that you were here that he wants."

"What on earth can it be?" Leslie wondered aloud. A horrifying thought struck her. "Do you suppose he thought we were in there, and he planned on—on murdering us while we slept?"

Duke looked down at her soberly. "I don't know what to think anymore. All I know is that it looks as if the man's getting desperate about something. One thing's for certain, though."

"What's that?"

"I'll be going with you to St. Louis. And you don't dare argue."

Leslie shook her head. "I won't!"

"Good. Well, we might as well be on our way. Since we didn't get any breakfast, why don't we pick up some milk and doughnuts at the grocery store? You can do that while I finish off with Bob and the officer."

In a matter of minutes, Leslie had purchased a carton of milk and a package of doughnuts, and they were under way. She went into the sleeper to pour each of them a glass of milk. The milk was in a cardboard carton, which bore on one side, as did so many of the milk cartons these days, a picture of a missing child, together with the child's name, age and place and date of disappearance. Leslie glanced at the picture briefly, then more closely. The child was a boy, and his name was Frederick Cliveden Phillips Marshall, missing from his home in Grosse Point, Michigan, since a year ago last January. It must be Cliveden Phillips's grandson!

She studied the slightly blurred picture carefully. The boy looked somewhat familiar. Had she, after all, seen the pictures in the newspapers when he was first reported missing? No, that didn't seem right. It was something else. Her body tensed as her mind seemed to be running multiple cross-checks at a fever pitch. She had seen a boy who looked like that, but from a different angle, at a distance... Suddenly it was like an explosion in her brain. She knew where it had been, and she was almost sure it was him!

"Duke!" she cried, pushing her way into the truck cab. "Pull over and stop right away! I've got something important to tell you."

Duke glanced at her, frowning.

"I'm only supposed to pull onto the shoulder here in case of an emergency."

"This is one, believe me! See this carton?" She waved the milk carton at Duke, who nodded. "Well, the Phillips boy's picture is on it, and I think I've seen him."

"My God, where?" Duke asked, slowing the truck quickly.

"Back at Hunt's Point. I may have a picture of him on one of the rolls of film I took."

Duke brought the truck to a stop and took the carton from Leslie's shaking hand.

"That's Clive's grandson all right. It's a great idea, putting pictures out like this. I only saw the child once. Otherwise, I wouldn't be sure of recognizing him." He looked at Leslie sharply. "Where was he when you think you saw him?"

"In the back of a truck quite a ways down the dock from yours. He only poked his head out a few times as they were unloading the truck, and the man he was with kept gesturing for him to get back inside. He was so cute, I tried to catch a picture of him as he looked out. That was the one I was shooting when you came up behind me and told me to get out of your way. I hurried it a little, but I think I probably caught him."

"As I recall, I said 'I beg your pardon,'" Duke said, wrinkling his forehead at her reprovingly. "Did you see what the man looked like?"

Leslie shook her head. "No. How I wish I had. All I know is they were unloading crates of lettuce. The man had on dark clothing, and his back was turned to me most of the time. But maybe if we enlarge the pictures, we'll be able to recognize something helpful, like the names on the crates."

Duke was silent, pulling on his chin thoughtfully, his eyes narrowed. He shook his head. "It could be. I can't imagine why or how, but in a way it fits. My God, how bizarre that would be."

"What?" Leslie cried, maddened by the uncommunicativeness of Duke's soliloquy.

"Callahan," Duke replied, looking at her but still almost looking through her. "You, your cameras. If he saw you taking pictures and he has the boy..."

"But why would he want him? You said no one asked for a ransom or responded to the rewards. And how could he hide him from Mr. Phillips? And why would he take him where you might see him? It doesn't make sense, Duke, except for the camera angle. If he thought I had pictures that would place him with the boy, it probably would make him come after me and my cameras, but the rest just doesn't fit."

Duke shook his head. "A lot of it certainly doesn't. But as for hiding him from me or Phillips, I seldom see the man, maybe twice a year, and never where he lives. The Phillips and their daughter and her husband live in

Michigan, two thousand miles from where Callahan lives. Clive visits the farms once in a while, but he doesn't frequent the kind of places where you'd find Callahan." He gave Leslie a penetrating look. "The problem now is where you can get the film developed fast. Any ideas?"

"I sure do," Leslie said with a positive nod. "Mr. Braemer Senior is a fine amateur photographer. I found out from my dancing partner that he did those pictures in the lobby of the inn. I'd bet my boots he's got a good darkroom."

Leslie's hunch was right, and Mr. Braemer enthusiastically lent both his darkroom and his help in developing her film. It did not take Duke more than a quick glance through a magnifying glass at the picture Leslie had mentioned to identify the man and the boy.

"That's Callahan, all right, and Freddie. At least the boy looks healthy enough." He paused. "Oh, dear God—" he looked at Leslie, stricken. "Remember the big bag I saw him carrying into the laundry at the truck stop?"

"Oh, Duke," Leslie felt a terrible chill go through her. "Was it . . . that big?" At Duke's nod she felt tears rush to her eyes. "What shall we do now? Call the police?"

Duke shook his head. "No, not yet. Let's operate on the assumption that the boy is still with him until we know differently, and pray that we're right. I'm afraid that, if Callahan saw police officers or even plain-clothes strangers approaching him, he'd panic, and as unstable as he must be, I don't think the boy would be safe. I think the best bet is for me to intercept him again, try to separate him from his truck somehow and put him out of commission so that I can get to the boy.

He won't be expecting anything from me, so the element of surprise should give me enough advantage to—"

"What's all this 'I' and 'me' business?" Leslie interrupted with a frown. "You don't have some dim-witted idea of trying to leave me behind, do you?"

"Leslie, I am not going to take you into what might be a very dangerous situation." As sparks started flying from Leslie's eyes, he smiled placatingly. "Besides, I don't know how long it will be before the right opportunity presents itself, and you do have to get to St. Louis, don't you? I'm sure that Mr. Braemer could help you arrange that." Duke looked questioningly at the innkeeper, who had been listening silently.

Leslie began seeing red. Before the man could reply, she snapped angrily, "St. Louis be damned, I'm going with you!" What right did Duke have to try to push her aside, like some helpless wimp? She was the one who had discovered the boy, wasn't she? "What's the matter? Do you want all the glory for finding the boy?"

"Leslie, you know damned well I don't!" Duke roared. "I don't want to have to worry about you! It's you and your pictures that Callahan's after!"

"Well, what about me worrying about you?" Leslie roared back. As Mr. Braemer flinched visibly, she softened her voice. "Besides, I think we'd do a lot better if we stuck together. This sounds like a two-person operation to me. You distract Callahan while I get the boy out of harm's way, or something like that."

Duke's mouth twisted as he chewed on his lip, looking from Leslie's face to Carl Braemer's, which was stolidly neutral.

"Stubborn woman," Duke remarked. "All right, come along. But don't say I didn't warn you, and for

God's sake, don't try to be some kind of superheroine.''

"As if I'd do that," Leslie said tightly, wishing that she hadn't mentioned some of her more disastrous childhood escapades that night when she'd had her nightmare. Duke's obvious real concern made her feel more vulnerable than she liked. Not only that, but she was deeply concerned for Duke's safety, too. Maybe there was something valid to be said against deep emotional involvements. Not that she could do anything about that now, she thought with a sigh.

They profusely thanked a now-anxious Carl Braemer, who made them promise to call him that evening so that he would know they were safe.

"Do you think it's likely that Callahan is waiting somewhere down the road for us?" Leslie asked as they started on their way. She had reluctantly agreed to retreat to the sleeper again in order to keep their quarry confused about whether she was now with Duke.

"I think the odds are heavily in favor of it. I doubt he'll think we'd connect the break-in with him. Of course there's always the chance he might have decided to head off into the mountains and hide. If he does that, even police with dogs and helicopters will have a devil of a time finding him. Our best hope is that he's so obsessed with finding those pictures that he keeps on looking for this truck and assuming that we're still together."

Duke fell silent for a while, and Leslie was left with her own muddled thoughts about fate and herself and Duke, and now the little boy who, she prayed, was all right. How different things would be for all of them if she hadn't driven about six blocks in a red Corvette one bright spring day.

So far, at least, everything was working out for the best, even Duke's rejection of her impetuous "I'll marry you" last night. The cold light of reality made her painfully aware now that she would have to be very sure of Duke's love and devotion before she said yes again. Just the thought of him sharing another woman's bed would tear her apart even more so now. She had been right all along, at least as far as she was concerned. The physical act of love was not something that could be separated from the total commitment of love and marriage. But would Duke ever come to feel that way about it? Somehow it just wouldn't be enough that he pay lip service to her ideals.

The sound of Duke's voice coming over the intercom startled her out of her ruminations, and his similar train of thought surprised her even more.

"Leslie," he said, "about last night. I really feel rotten about what happened. It was unforgivable of me, taking advantage of you like that when I knew how you felt about the importance of being married before you had sex. My one excuse, and it isn't a very good one, is that I was overtired, and my usual self-discipline broke down. I'd apologize, but it seems a pretty inadequate thing to do under the circumstances."

Leslie found herself staring in the direction of Duke's voice. Had she heard him right? Did he really think it was all his doing, that she had put up no resistance because he had her so mesmerized that she couldn't? She had seen her surrender coming for days, it seemed, knowing subconsciously that her love for him made it inevitable. But Duke didn't see it that way. He thought only of uncontrollable physical desires having destroyed her ability to resist. Oh, he had asked if she'd changed her mind but obviously did not take her response as an affirmative answer.

She frowned as another set of alternatives occurred to her. Was Duke being extremely gentlemanly in taking all of the blame, or could it be that he was trying to tell her that, now that he'd thought it over, it hadn't been so great after all, and he wished he hadn't made himself feel the least bit obligated by taking her virginity. She felt a tiny seed of anger start sprouting in the middle of an unpleasant ache in her chest. If so, why didn't he just come right out and say that, whatever the result to his political ambitions, he wasn't so sure anymore that it was worth losing his freedom?

The last thing she needed was his apology. She'd wanted him, and she had no regrets on that score. She now had a real measure of the kind of pleasure that sex should bring. For once, she felt, something she had blundered into had turned out right. Duke could just take his apology and stuff it.

"I didn't hear me complaining," she replied coolly. "Did you? In fact, I distinctly recall having told you I'd marry you and your telling me to shut up and go to sleep, which I did. Subject closed."

"Except for one thing," Duke said.

"What's that?"

"Well, I was wondering, since you're a rather... atypical case, were you using any protection? I know I wasn't."

Thunderstruck, Leslie thought rapidly. Good Lord, she might have gotten pregnant! No wonder Duke was worried! He would be concerned about her. He wasn't the kind of man who wouldn't be. But he might also be terrified that he'd gotten himself into a real trap! She couldn't have him thinking that. She still wanted desperately for him to love her, to want to marry her, but not for him to feel he had to do so. How fortunate that he'd at least had the presence of mind to reject her offer to marry him last night. Or maybe that was what had brought him to his senses! He hadn't really realized how close to the edge he was skating.

"Of course I was," she replied, hoping her pause hadn't been too obviously long. "What kind of a dummy do you think I am?"

"I don't think you're a dummy at all," Duke replied with what sounded to Leslie like a relieved chuckle. "It occurred to me that that might have had something to do with your sudden decision to marry me."

"No, it was a simple case of insanity," Leslie said tartly.

And now they were back to square one. Or maybe square zero. But she was not going to say a word now about whether Duke's proposal was still open. Let him bring that up and try to wriggle out of it if he wanted to. It would give her some small bit of grim satisfaction to watch him do it, and even more to tell him that it didn't really matter because she'd decided she couldn't marry him after all. Unless Duke proposed to her for the right reasons, her answer would have to be no.

"So it's back to no again this morning?" Duke asked, reflecting her thoughts.

Oh, dear. Leslie clenched her hands, feeling her entire body grow tense.

"I'm afraid so," she answered slowly, wondering if it wouldn't be both kinder and safer to tell him that she really couldn't think about marriage on his terms but failing to find the courage to do so. But then, maybe she wouldn't have to. "Why?" she asked in a timid voice.

"I just wondered," Duke replied.

His voice was so neutral that Leslie wished desperately that she could see his face. Maybe he was having trouble finding the courage to tell her...

"Hello, who's that behind us?" Duke's voice now sounded tense. "I wonder where he came from?"

Leslie knew it must be Callahan's truck that had appeared.

"What do we do now?" she asked. "Where are we?"

"Not far from highway 40. I'll find a decent-looking place to stop for some coffee and see if Callahan stops and makes his usual attempt to strike up a conversation. I'll mention the break-in last night and see how cool he is about it. That will give me some indication of the state of mind he's in. I'd like to have some idea of that before I decide what to do next."

"What if he asks about me?"

"I'll just keep telling him I don't know what he's talking about, as I have been."

"The future congressman issues another denial," Leslie said in pompous tones. "And what am I supposed to do?"

"Nothing, yet," Duke replied.

"Humph," Leslie sniffed. "Why do I have the feeling you're going to keep telling me that?"

"I can't imagine. I'll have something for you to do when I've got a plan. Now just sit tight, and don't get impatient," Duke said firmly. "We have to think first about the boy's safety."

"Yes, sir," Leslie said. "But I keep thinking about how he must feel, too. Do you suppose Callahan has harmed him?"

"If he has..."

Duke did not finish his statement. Shortly he slowed the truck, and Leslie knew he must have found a place to stop.

"Callahan's running true to form," he said when he had parked the truck. "He's right beside us, not five feet away. I can see I'm not going to be denied the pleasure of his company."

Leslie chewed on her knuckles for a few minutes after Duke had left, feeling terribly frustrated. There must be something she could do besides this eternal sitting and waiting. Perhaps she could peer into Callahan's truck and see if there was any sign of a child's recent presence. If it was only five feet away...

Cautiously she opened the compartment door and peered out. The shabby-looking truck next to them was parked between Duke's truck and the restaurant. It was an ideal chance for her to investigate without being seen. She probably had at least ten minutes before she needed to worry about anyone coming back. In seconds she had let herself out and had climbed up to look in the window of the Phillips Farms truck cab. It was littered with cigarette wrappers, old lunch bags and tools.

Then she saw something that made her heart beat faster. Slung over the steering wheel was a shoulder holster and gun. Callahan wasn't carrying it with him! If she could get to it first, Duke wouldn't have to worry about anything but Callahan's fists, and she would bet on Duke being able to handle him. But was the boy in there? She could see nothing that would indicate that he was.

She tried the door, shaking it vigorously but futilely. It was locked. How she wished right now that she really did know how to deal with locks as Duke had once suspected! Feeling anxious and frustrated, she was about to go back when she thought she heard a whimpering sound coming from the small sleeping compartment. It must be like a sardine can in there, she thought, leaning closer and listening intently. The sound grew louder, and then she head a little voice saying words that made her heart feel as if it would actually break.

"Is that you, Spike? I'm hungry. Did you bring me something? Spike? Can you hear me? I want something to eat. I'll be good. I won't get out of the sleeper again. I promise."

Oh, no! The child wasn't even being fed regularly! He was being starved as punishment for leaving his windowless prison and risking someone seeing him, no doubt a worry brought on by the new milk-carton picture. Leslie felt such a surge of hatred for the man named Callahan whom she had never met, but who had caused so much trouble, that she thought she would explode. How dare he mistreat the child? She reached over and tapped on the sleeper.

"Freddie, is that you? Can you hear me?"

There was a silence for a moment, and then a little voice replied, "Yeah, my name's Freddie. Who's there? How'd you know?"

"I'm a friend. My name is Leslie. I'm with Duke Caldwell. He's a friend of your grandfather's." Or at least he would be if they got Freddie out of this safely. "We're going to help you," she said.

"Whatcha going to do?"

"I'm not sure yet, but we'll get you back to your family soon. Try to be brave a little longer. And don't let Mr. Callahan know I've talked to you."

"But I wanta get out of here now!" cried the voice, and then a little head appeared through the opening of the small sleeper and peered out at Leslie, tearful blue eyes huge in a pale, gaunt face below a thatch of unkempt blond hair. "Can't you get the door open?"

Oh, dear, Leslie thought, *now what do I do!* She shook her head. "Can you unlock it from in there?"

The boy shook his head. "He's fixed it so I can't."

He came the rest of the way into the cab and pressed his freckled nose to the window, his eyes so wistful and yet full of hope that Leslie's heart melted completely. She couldn't let him down. Somehow she had to get him out of there and do it in less than five minutes. But how? After only a few seconds of thought, she concluded that there was only one way. She would have to break the window so that Freddie could climb out.

"Tell you what, Freddie," she said, "I'm going to have to break the window. I'll get a big wrench from our truck right behind me and do it. You get back in the sleeper so the glass doesn't cut you. Okay? And as soon as it's done, you can climb out and get into our truck with me. We've got lots of good things to eat over there."

"Okay, as soon as you get the wrench," Freddie replied.

Poor child, he didn't even believe it would happen, Leslie thought as she vaulted into Duke's truck and grabbed a huge wrench from the cab floor. As soon as Freddie saw her returning, he smiled and disappeared, and Leslie swung at the heavy safety glass with all her might. It took several blows to clear enough away from the opening to make it safe for the boy to climb through without too much danger of glass cutting him, but as soon as she had done so, Leslie called to Freddie, and he came hurrying to the opening. She was just lifting him out in her arms when she saw, through the other windows of the truck, that Callahan and Duke were returning and that she had been seen. She saw Callahan start running toward them and Duke lunge after him, but she had no time to watch what happened after that.

"Call the police!" she yelled at another trucker, who was watching the scene in amazement, as she thrust Freddie ahead of her into Duke's truck. "Stay down and crawl into the sleeper," she told him as she pulled the door shut behind her, locked it and followed him into the rear compartment.

"Phew! That was exciting, wasn't it?" she said, smiling at the boy while she listened anxiously for any sound that would indicate that Spike Callahan had managed to get back to his truck and his gun.

"Yeah, you're neat," said Freddie, smiling back at her.

I doubt if Duke will think so, Leslie thought, beginning to relax as there was no unpleasant sound from without. Well, she would deal with his displeasure at her precipitate rescue later. She had a hungry little boy on her hands who needed to feel that he was back with people who cared for him. They were sitting on the floor between the bunk and the refrigerator. She put an arm around Freddie and hugged him close, then leaned forward, opened the refrigerator door and took out the fateful carton of milk she had purchased only hours before. She held it up so that Freddie could see his picture.

"Did you know that you were famous?" she asked him.

CHAPTER TEN

LESLIE STOOD ALONE, lost in thought, staring out at the lights of Memphis far below from the window of Loren Barstow's suite. So much had happened. Soon there would be a telephone call from the pilot of the Phillips's private jet, which was being loaned to her by the grateful family to take her to St. Louis so that she would be able to keep her appointment in the morning. It was as if she had lived an entire separate lifetime in just four days, one that was completely unconnected to her real life and that was now over. Had the red Corvette been like Aladdin's lamp, her very touching of it magically triggering the incredible series of events? Whatever the answer, she was grateful. Although her heart ached, and probably would for a long, long time, she would not have missed her days with Duke Caldwell for anything. But, especially, she was glad for the little boy now asleep in his father's arms and for a much older boy who had held his mother close while tears sparkled on his thick black lashes.

"Ah, there you are." Loren's resonant voice permeated the room as he entered and came to Leslie's side, a fatherly smile creasing his distinguished face. "Taking a little respite? It must have been a tiring day for you."

Leslie nodded. "I've already said my goodbyes. It's a family gathering in there," she said, referring to the suite next door, which Cliveden Phillips and his wife, Duke's mother, were occupying with their son-in-law and grandson. "I'm so glad that Duke and his mother are talking to each other."

"So am I. I've tried for years to convince that stubborn rascal to make the first move toward a reconciliation. Nothing good ever comes of refusing to communicate."

"That's more or less what I told Duke, too," Leslie said. "My intuition told me there was probably a side to his mother's story that he didn't know." She looked up at the tall lawyer. "Was there, do you know?"

"Most definitely. But, of course, it's privileged information."

"Of course. I only wanted to know if my hunch was right," Leslie said quickly.

"Perhaps Duke will tell you when he knows," Loren said. "You deserve to have your curiosity satisfied. If it weren't for you, I'm not sure what might have brought them together."

"Oh, it wasn't my doing," Leslie protested. "It was a red Corvette." At the questioning lift of Loren's bushy brows, she smiled and gave him a sketchy version of her whimsical theory, including her accident and the real reason she had been in Duke's truck in the first place. There seemed no reason to pretend any longer.

Loren fixed Leslie with the penetrating look that had earned him his nickname and remarked casually, "I was wondering what that cock-and-bull story about you two being engaged was all about. Why don't we sit down and have a little drink while you tell me about it? It will probably be a while before the plane is ready, and I think you need to have a sympathetic ear."

"You mean you—you never believed us at all?" Leslie asked, amazed, as she accepted a snifter of brandy and sank into a luxuriously soft chair.

The eminent lawyer chuckled. "I do make my living by knowing what people are thinking but not saying, you know. Of course, Duke is fairly easy to read, and he looked as if he'd just swallowed a dose of strong medicine. However—" he shrugged "—I could see that you two had a compelling reason for wanting that story believed, so I did what I could, in spite of what the police officers told me about some message on a bathroom wall. I still haven't been able to reconcile that with your being on Callahan's trail and not wanting it known. Or isn't that what was going on?"

"No, not at the time," Leslie said. "We weren't on his trail until this morning. He was on ours. Duke thought he was part of a scheme that Cliveden Phillips had set up to discredit him with the voters in his district, since he'd already tried something like that once." She went on to explain Duke's worry over his reputation and his suspicions about her mission. "And the engagement almost did come to pass," she concluded. "Duke was sure you'd tell the first reporter you saw, and he practically ordered me to follow through so that my trip with him would look legitimate."

Loren Barstow shook his shaggy mane of white hair. "I don't know why it is that bachelors his age become so involved in the cleverness of their intrigues. It becomes a game to them. My son, Aaron, is the same way. The contortions he goes through to try to deceive his mother and me are almost laughable. I suppose it is preferable to his having a reputation as a wild womanizer, and Duke is right that such a reputation would damage his chances at the polls, but I doubt that having you along on one trip could have done that much damage." He stared at Leslie thoughtfully. "So you turned him down. Why? You love him."

Leslie almost choked on her brandy. No wonder this man could extract reluctant confessions from criminals!

"Is it . . . that obvious?" she asked hoarsely.

"To me it is. Maybe not to Duke. He's used to dealing with women who are just as interested in being devious as he is. But he is a fine man, one of the kindest and most generous I've ever known."

"I know that," Leslie said, her eyes blurring as she looked into her brandy glass. "But I'm afraid the love is one-sided. Maybe Duke has had too many years of playing those games. I think it all started because he was so bitter about his mother." She sighed heavily. "He said if I'd marry him, he'd follow all the rules of being a good husband, but that's just not enough for me to commit myself for life."

"I can certainly understand that. But Duke is in love with you, you know. Very deeply. Although he's probably not aware of it yet. I wouldn't despair, Leslie. It may take him a while to realize it, but perhaps getting back with his mother may help him along the path. You'll be hearing from him with a real proposal one of these days." He smiled as Leslie gazed at him dubiously, blinking back her tears. "I'll wager you a new press photo every year for the next ten years that I'm right. If I lose, I'll pay double your regular price."

"All right, but it seems a bit odd to take a bet that I hope I'll lose," Leslie agreed, managing a little smile.

The telephone rang, and Leslie gathered herself for the news that the airplane was ready. When Loren stayed on the phone for quite a long time, she relaxed again.

"That was an enlightening call," Loren said as he returned to his chair. "It seems that Mr. Callahan finally made a complete statement, and now the mystery of why he abducted young Frederick in the first place is solved. Spike Callahan is, in reality, a fellow named Lawrence Biggs, who was fired from a junior executive position in the accounting department of International Enterprises for some kind of tax fraud. He couldn't find another job and subsequently was divorced by his attractive young wife. He blamed Cliveden Phillips for his troubles and decided to do whatever he could to make his life miserable. Since he'd lived in the Detroit area and knew of Phillips's devotion to his grandson, he hatched the plot to adopt a new identity and get a trucking job with the very company that had fired him, and then make a quick trip to Michigan to snatch the boy. He planned eventually to have an accomplice return Freddie and collect the reward for the two of them to share, but only after he figured that Phillips had suffered as much as he had. God only knows how long he thought that might take."

"If that isn't bizarre!" Leslie exclaimed. "He didn't sound like anyone who could have been an executive, although he did look a little like one. Shouldn't you go and tell the others?"

Loren shrugged. "When you've gone will be soon enough. Tell me what you've heard from your father lately."

They chatted a while longer, and then the telephone rang again, this time with the expected news that the plane was waiting.

"I don't know how to thank you for everything, Loren," Leslie said as he ushered her into his limousine for the trip to the airport. "Without your help we'd probably still be stuck over there in Arkansas with everyone running around in circles, not knowing quite what to do about the boy, or getting his family here, or anything. It's certainly lucky you were still in Memphis."

"It's probably that red Corvette again," Loren said with a chuckle. "I was supposed to have gone on to Nashville, but an old friend persuaded me to stay over and talk to his students at the university." He held Leslie's hand as she sat in the back seat of the limousine, and bent to give her a quick kiss on the cheek. "Remember what I told you, and keep your chin up," he said. "Duke will come around."

"Don't you say anything, Loren," Leslie warned.

Loren Barstow smiled and raised both of his famous eyebrows at the same time, looking positively devilish.

"Nothing obvious," he agreed as he closed the door and signaled to the chauffeur to depart.

Leslie settled back, shaking her head in bemused wonder as they sped away. This was a fitting ending, she thought, being driven to the airport in the most elegant limousine she'd ever seen in order to board a private jet, doubtless not short on elegance, either, and carrying in her purse a huge check from a grateful Cliveden Phillips, who absolutely refused to take no for an answer. Only one thing was missing from this fairy-tale adventure—the happy ending. Could Loren be right? He was so perceptive, and yet Duke had not seemed to her that afternoon like a man in love.

Once Callahan was in custody, neatly subdued by Duke's skillful tackle, which had dropped him like a felled tree onto the hard pavement, she had expected Duke to tell her in no uncertain terms what he thought of her impetuous decision to free the boy immediately. He had not. He had been warm and gentle with little Freddie, calming him as doctors examined him and found him quite well except for his emotional trauma. To her, Duke had seemed a trifle . . . well, distant, as if he were somehow looking at her differently. She had been sure that something had changed when he made no mention of their supposed engagement when he introduced her to his mother and the rest of Freddie's family, letting them think that her sole reason for accompanying him had been to track down Freddie's abductor. She had guessed then that he must have taken Loren aside and told him the engagement wasn't real. Apparently he hadn't been able to muster the courage to tell her that his proposal was off, although she would have guessed the truth when it became obvious that everyone believed she had accompanied him in order to find Callahan and Freddie.

Of course, he'd had a lot on his mind, what with seeing his mother for the first time in fifteen years and having to deal with Cliveden Phillips, who suddenly wanted to be his friend instead of his enemy. There had really been no time for them to be alone and talk. Perhaps it was no wonder that he had only briefly embraced her and kissed her on the forehead when they said goodbye. At the time she had thought bitterly that he was merely reinforcing the idea that they were nothing more than friends who had cooperated on the capture of Spike Callahan. But maybe he was also giving her a message, something like the infamous Don't call me, I'll call you.

She was sure of it by the end of the week in St. Louis, a week during which she found her emotions very hard to control. She kept remembering Duke's "Oh, *that* Molly," and picturing him standing beside the luscious brunette as Leslie peered at the model through her viewfinder, wondering just how well he knew her and what on earth he could have seen in the vicious bitch. Everyone else had responded with praise and admiration when they read of Leslie's role in rescuing young Frederick Marshall in the brief press release Loren had issued on the family's behalf. Molly persisted in calling Leslie "our heroine" and asking her how she could have come out of that adventure without any more interest from Duke Caldwell than she appeared to have.

"If I'd spent a couple of days in that truck with him, he'd have been camped on my doorstep for weeks afterward," Molly remarked during one break while the makeup man applied some extra blusher to her pallid cheeks so that she would look healthy enough to display the latest outdoor apparel.

Leslie saw red. "Maybe it's because we were both more interested in someone else's welfare," she snapped. "Of course, I wouldn't expect you to understand that, you self-centered, empty-headed clotheshorse."

The makeup man's hand jerked and he sketched a reddish slash across the model's chin as he burst out laughing, drawing a fit of temper from Molly, which took several minutes to calm.

Leslie stood stonily, not in the least sorry for having made up a bit of a story in order to deliver her message. Molly richly deserved it, and it helped a little to relieve the terrible tension Leslie had built up, lying awake in her hotel room night after night, wishing that

the telephone would ring and wondering what would
have happened if Duke hadn't rejected her one accep-
tance of his proposal. Would he have backed out after
they found Freddie? Or would he have felt compelled to
go through with a loveless marriage? Which would she
prefer? She was beginning to think that anything would
be preferable to this aching void where her heart used
to be.

It will be better when I get back to New York, she told
herself as she waited in line at the airline ticket counter
on Saturday morning.

"Miss Leslie Lyon, please come to the information
booth in the blue concourse," a voice announced over
the speaker system.

"I wonder what that could be about," Leslie muttered to herself as she looked around, trying to orient
herself about which direction to go. "Lord, I hope
nothing's happened to Dad or Mother." Feeling more
anxious than ever, she got her bearings and hurried off.

"I'm Leslie Lyon," she breathlessly told the young
man in the booth when she reached her destination.

"Oh, yes." He smiled pleasantly and reached below
his counter. "This is for you," he said, handing her a
red, white and blue airline ticket envelope.

Leslie stared blankly at the envelope for a moment.
"For me? But I haven't . . . bought any ticket."

"I guess someone's bought one for you," said the
information attendant with a smile. "Why don't you
open it?"

"Oh, yes." Leslie nodded, feeling a strange premoni-
tory tingling as she did so. She pulled out the ticket and
quickly flipped open the cover to read the computer-
printed itinerary. She was to leave for San Diego in
about an hour, she found, flying first-class. There was

also a slip of paper with a typed message: "I will meet you at the airport. Duke."

"Oh, my goodness," Leslie breathed, clutching at the information counter for support. "I'd forgotten—"

"Are you all right?" the attendant asked anxiously.

"I'm not sure," Leslie replied. Her head was spinning drunkenly, her mind running off in several directions at once. She had, she had really forgotten that Duke had said she should come to California when she was through with her job in St. Louis. But that had been before... Did this mean his proposal was still open? And if it did, what on earth was she going to do?

CHAPTER ELEVEN

"I THOUGHT I was coming home, too, Melody, but I'm going to California instead," Leslie said irritably. "Yes, I know it's sudden, but I just found out myself. I just called to let you know and tell you I've put a check for you in the mail."

Why did life have to be so full of picky details? Making the decision to use the ticket already had her shaking. All she wanted to do now was get on the plane, quickly, before she had too much time to think. An announcement over the speaker system ended her dilemma.

"Melody, they're boarding the plane now. I've got to run. I'll call you as soon as I know something definite about . . . anything."

Clutching her camera bag and the small carryon she had purchased, Leslie was soon seated in the luxury of the first-class compartment of the DC-10. Thank goodness, she thought as she looked around at her elegant fellow passengers, she had put on the lovely new teal-blue cashmere sweater and matching skirt she had bought at the hotel boutique. Blue jeans definitely would have been out of place here, as well as not being what she would have wanted to be wearing to see Duke again. At that thought she leaned her head back and closed her eyes, gripping the arms of her seat tightly.

Hurry up and get this thing in the air, she mentally instructed the pilot, *before I lose my nerve.*

"Afraid of flying?" her seatmate asked sympathetically, seeing Leslie's white knuckles.

"Not at all," she replied, knowing he probably thought she was a terrible liar. It was what was awaiting her at the end of the trip that had her terrified. It might be anything from heaven to hell for her. She had to find out. There was no way she could figure it out until she saw Duke. Had Loren been right? Was she?

"Do you play gin rummy?" her seatmate asked as soon as the flight attendant had announced that the pilot had turned off the No Smoking sign.

I must look like a nervous wreck, Leslie thought, giving the pleasant-looking elderly man a weak smile. "Sure," she replied. Anything to keep her from dithering fruitlessly for the next three hours.

She had another weak smile for the flight attendant who cheerily instructed her to have a nice day as she left the plane. She picked Duke out of the waiting crowd instantly, his dark head inches taller than most of the people's there. He spotted her and came toward her, women staring at him as Leslie knew they always would at the handsome man, as striking in his ivory open-necked sports shirt and dark blue slacks as most men would be in a tuxedo.

"Hello, Leslie," he said softly, his brief welcoming smile not quite what she had hoped for, his face seeming taut, as if his nerves, too, were drawn tight. "I wasn't sure you'd come."

"I wasn't sure I would, either," she confessed, feeling less certain all the time that she should have. Was he so on edge because he had guessed that she loved him, and he didn't know how to tell her? With that terrifying thought sending fingers of ice through her, she walked along beside him as he silently took her baggage from her and led her to the parking lot where he opened the door of a red Porsche.

"At least it isn't a Corvette," she remarked shakily to break the silence.

Duke looked startled for a moment, then nodded. "Your sister's car," he said. He got in. "I thought we'd go somewhere where we could talk," he said. "It's not far. Just across the bridge to the Harbor Island Marina. I've borrowed a friend's offshore cruiser."

Leslie nodded, not sure she could trust herself to say anything. Maybe Loren thought that Duke was easy to read, but she was having no luck at all, her dilemma as great as ever. Why didn't Duke just come out with it? Why take her out on some boat?

Instead of answering her unspoken questions, he asked the banal, "Have a nice flight?"

Have a nice flight! Leslie scowled. No! she hadn't had a nice flight! What on earth was going on? She couldn't take much more of this. She had already put in four miserable hours, plus the week in St. Louis, mulling over her relationship with Duke Caldwell. Now it seemed as if he were determined to play cat and mouse for a while longer. Damn the man!

"No," she snapped in reply to his question, "it was perfectly miserable."

"What was wrong?" Duke asked, glancing over at her with a startled look. "Rough weather?"

"Only for me," Leslie growled. "I was standing in line to buy my ticket to New York when suddenly I found that I already had a ticket to San Diego. Couldn't you have called? I had no idea you still wanted me to come out here, and I still don't know why you did. I wish you'd stop playing games and tell me what this is all about."

"In a few minutes," Duke replied, staring straight ahead, the line of his jaw uncompromising and hard-looking.

And it was only minutes later that he turned into a parking lot and stopped next to a low stuccoed building. He came around to help Leslie from the car and then hurried her through some gates and down a dock where dozens of magnificent cruisers and sailing yachts were tied.

"Here we are," he said, turning her to walk alongside an immense boat that looked large enough to cruise the world. A small gangway was down; a tanned young man in brief white shorts waited at the top. "All set to go, Danny?" Duke asked him.

"You bet, Mr. Caldwell," the man answered.

"Go where?" Leslie asked, stopping and digging in her heels as she detected the sound of the boat's engines idling. Now what kind of a trip was Duke planning to take her on? Halfway across the United States in his truck had only succeeded in turning what had once been a fairly well-organized life into one of utter confusion! "I am not getting on that boat until I know what this is all about!"

"Wrong," Duke said, his voice deep and husky. "You won't find out until you get on the boat." As Leslie scowled at him, he suddenly grinned at her, his eyes sparkling with their old devilish mischief. "If you won't come quietly, I guess I'll just have to take you aboard like one of those pirates of old. Heave ho, my lassie, or whatever is appropriate." He picked Leslie up and flung her across his shoulder like a sack of flour.

"Cast off the lines, mate," he said to Danny as he bounded onto the boat.

"Put me down, damn it!" Leslie cried out in his ear.

Across the deck, down a short flight of stairs and into a spacious salon Duke carried Leslie, depositing her on the floor near a built-in lounge upholstered in plum-covered velvet, and then returning to close and lock the door behind him.

"Now I have you where I want you," Duke announced, advancing on Leslie with a wild gleam in his eyes, "and this time you're not getting away from me until I find out how you stole from me what you did and what you intend to do about it."

He's gone berserk again, Leslie thought, her wide eyes locked onto his and her heart thumping. *He's got some crazy new idea about something I'm supposed to be involved in!*

"What on earth are you talking about?" she cried. "I didn't take anything from you! There wasn't any-thing—" She choked to a stop as Duke clamped his hands down on her shoulders and peered into her eyes, sparks flying toward her from the depths of his own, which seemed now as black and shining as obsidian. She could almost feel an electric charge emanating from him.

"Don't play the innocent with me again," he rasped throatily. "You can't fool me anymore with those huge green eyes that look as guileless as a baby's. You had the robbery all planned out, didn't you? All the rest—your hiding away in the sleeper, pretending you were only interested in hiring me for some ridiculous job—were only distractions, so I wouldn't notice you doing it." He gave Leslie a little shake. "When did you manage to do it? It's more than I can figure out. I can't even remember anymore when I first began to suspect it was missing. I did think that I might find out that it wasn't missing after all when I got home, but I was wrong. It was nowhere to be found. And now that I have you here, I know for certain where it is. You have it.''

Leslie's eyes grew misty as she stared at that incredibly handsome face so close to hers. She loved him so. It didn't matter what he thought of her—she would always love him. There must be something she could do to help him out of his confusion. It was terribly sad. Poor Duke had really gone over the edge this time.

"Maybe I—I didn't mean to do it,'' she stammered hoarsely. "If you'd just give me some more clues—'' She ground to a halt again. Why was he looking at her so strangely? Why was he starting to smile, as if he were not really angry with her at all... What was she missing here?

Then suddenly his arms enveloped her, and she felt that familiar warmth that only his closeness could give her penetrate her trembling body, as he held her so tightly against his own tensely hard muscles that she could scarcely breathe. She felt his cheek against her hair, heard him murmur her name over and over as his hands traveled up and down as if they were trying to make sure that she was real.

There'd been another time like this, she thought, her arms going around him, her cheek burrowing against the silky shirt, her arms clutching his broad back, her every sense responding joyfully, even though her mind was still in turmoil. She could feel the fast, strong beating of his heart. He must care about her, even if he did think she was some kind of a thief. It couldn't be anything terribly important.

Suddenly Leslie froze. Everything in that seething, disorganized confusion that had once been a neatly functioning brain dropped into place like the pieces of a puzzle, with a jolt that left her breathless. Duke's heart! That was what he was talking about! That was what he meant! She jerked her head back and stared up into a pair of laughing brown eyes.

"Finally figured it out, did you?" he chuckled.

"You devil!" she cried. "You mean, rotten—"

There was a long interruption while Duke silenced Leslie's complaints with a kiss that sent every doubt flying and left her feverish with desire. She swayed dizzily with the rocking of the boat, clinging to Duke for support as at last he raised his head.

"Let's check out the captain's cabin," he said huskily, lifting her in his arms and carrying her down a little passageway and into a room with dark mahogany walls, soft lights and a sumptuous bed covered in pale pink satin.

"Oh, Duke, even satin sheets?" Leslie murmured as he lay her carefully down and then stretched out beside her.

"My friend believes in pleasure cruising," he said, giving her one of his mischievous winks. "I used to, too."

"And now?" Leslie asked, her hands moving to begin unbuttoning his shirt. "Isn't this for pleasure?"

"Not the same kind," he replied, giving a deep groaning sigh as Leslie pulled his shirt free and proceeded to kiss him from his neck to his navel while one hand investigated the extent of his arousal. "Just a darn minute, Miss Lyon," he said, capturing her hand and holding it before she could unfasten his belt. "There's something I want to ask you before we get past the point of talking.''

"Ask away," she said, leaning on one elbow and caressing his face with her hand, adoring the strong lines and vivid coloring that were such a perfect reflection of the exciting man within. The scamp! She knew now what he was going to ask, and her heart beat faster in anticipation.

"Will you marry me? Marry me for no other reason than that I love you and want you and could never imagine any other woman being a part of me as you already are? I know it's been a very short time, and you may still have some doubts..."

Leslie shook her head and placed a finger on his lips. "No doubts. I love you, and I'd almost decided I'd marry you no matter what you felt, I was so miserable without you. But I would like to know what happened to make you change your mind so quickly. If it doesn't take too long to tell, that is," she added, brushing her lips against his.

"It wasn't so much changing my mind as it was letting myself believe that what I felt was really love. I tried to fight it. Even after that first day I found you in my truck I was fighting it, but it was too strong and too different for me to deny." He grinned and tickled Leslie's cheek before beginning to unbutton her sweater. "I thought I was so clever, figuring I could marry you and still keep from making a total commitment. I knew I couldn't stand the idea of another man having you. But it wasn't long before I knew that there was no way I could tolerate the idea of you having a marriage that was something less than the one you wanted. That was why I couldn't let you say yes that night, not just because I knew your judgment was definitely clouded. I was on the horns of a dilemma, knowing all the signs were pointing the one way I was terrified to go. Then when you rescued Freddie, you were so magnificent—"

"Magnificent?" Leslie squeaked. "I was sure you'd be furious with me. I never could figure out how you felt about that."

"Amazed and relieved. I'd already decided there was no way I was going to let Callahan get back in his truck. He was a man on the verge of doing something desperate. All I could think of doing was starting a fight and hoping I could knock him out before some do-gooder stopped us, but when he saw you and broke and ran, it gave me a chance to use one of my best open-field tackles. There was no way on God's earth I was going to let him get near you. Too bad you didn't see it." Duke grinned and insinuated his hand beneath Leslie's bra. "You'd have been proud of the old man."

"I'm sure I would have," Leslie said, her voice muffled in the pillow as she turned so that Duke could unfasten the clasp. She heard him catch a deep, rasping breath as she turned back over, his eyes and then his lips caressing her breasts. "The rest . . . of your story?" she whispered.

"Oh, that," Duke said with an exaggerated sigh. He sat up and flung his shirt aside and then lay back down to pull Leslie close against him. "Suddenly the world looked very different. I saw possibilities I'd never seen before. I saw a woman of courage and daring who meant more to me than life itself instead of just an adorable little kook who did wild and wonderful things. I wondered if that was what your kind of love meant. And then, when I saw my mother again, it was as if a dam had burst. It was wonderful and frightening at the same time. I learned that you were right, that my mother did have a story to tell, one I might not have wanted to hear if it weren't for you. She and my father had been at odds for years, he denying her any chance to get the education she craved or even take a part-time job. Nothing was as simple as I'd thought, especially when it came to you and me. I was going to have to give you a genuine proposal and—God help my bachelor soul—admit that I was in love with you. I was just beginning to realize that when I let you go in Memphis, but I thought I'd better wait a bit and see what happened when we were apart. Everything had been so intense I didn't trust myself. As you can tell, it didn't take me long to become sure of how I felt. Then I started worrying about you. I wanted to believe Loren—''

"He promised not to tell!" Leslie cried, lifting her head from its cradle in the curve of Duke's shoulder.

"Are you sorry he did?" Duke asked, smiling as Leslie shook her head. "He's just a matchmaker at heart. He told me what fine people your parents are, how he's known you since you were a little girl. I knew he was leading up to something, so I asked him outright. For once he didn't try any evasion. But I still needed to hear it from you. Say it again, hmmm?"

"I love you," Leslie said, feeling a great surge of happiness at the answering light in Duke's eyes. "And now, my love, what are we going to do? I mean, after we spend a few hours making love."

"I thought we might cruise around for a couple of days, soak up some sun and pretend the rest of the world doesn't exist. How does that sound?"

"Heavenly. How about a couple of years instead?"

Duke chuckled. "Would that we could. But we have a wedding to plan, I have a campaign to work on and you, as I recall, have to keep an appointment in El Salvador soon.''

Leslie could feel him tense as he mentioned El Salvador. The idea did not sound very appealing to her now, either. It could be quite dangerous, something that hadn't bothered her when she had only herself to think of.

"I think I'll skip El Salvador," she said thoughtfully. "I'll find someone to take my place."

"Really?" Duke sounded relieved. "I don't want to interfere with your career," he added quickly.

"Don't worry, I won't let you," Leslie said archly, giggling as Duke tickled her and then began removing the rest of their clothing. "You know," she said as he finished and then pulled her over to lie on top of him, "I did tell you a bit of a whopper the other day."

"What was that?" Duke's hands molded her back and bottom, making her shiver with delight.

"I didn't really use any protection. I don't even have any. We might have…started something the other night. Do you mind?"

Duke cocked a black eyebrow at her. "Only might have?"

Leslie nodded.

"Do you want to?"

"Oh, yes." Leslie nodded again.

"Then we'd better make sure." Duke smiled, a wonderful combination of love and happiness and mischief that made Leslie's heart sing with joy. "I believe this is a necessary first step toward getting those grandchildren you'll need to tell our story to."

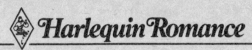
Harlequin Romance

Coming Next Month

2827 TIME TO TRUST Rosemary Badger
A reporter on vacation in Australia saves her new neighbor's son from drowning. And instead of thanks she gets a tongue-lashing! What on earth could make a man so distrustful?

2828 EARTHLY TREASURES Sarah Keene
What starts out as a weekend visit to her sister in Sequoia National Park ends in a broken engagement—and a disturbing attraction to a naturalist who seems more comfortable with wildlife than he does with her.

2829 CONTRASTS Rowan Kirby
A ceramic potter's orderly life in Somerset is thrown into disarray when an irresistible veterinarian makes her realize there's more to life than work—much more!

2830 O'HARA'S LEGACY Leigh Michaels
First came the surprise of having inherited a bookstore, then the shock of having to share it with a perfect stranger—so perfect, in fact, that she wants the partnership to become permanently binding.

2831 A TALENT FOR LOVING Celia Scott
The chance to be near a movie star idol prompts a young Toronto woman to work for a fiery-tempered photographer who quickly outshines his famous friend in every way. If only he knew it!

2832 DIAMOND VALLEY Margaret Way
An orphan, raised as one of the family in a wealthy Australian outback clan, finds herself alluring marriage material when one-third of the Diamond Valley ranch becomes hers. And she's heartsick!

Available in April wherever paperback books are sold, or through Harlequin Reader Service.

In the U.S.
P.O. Box 1397
Buffalo, N.Y.
14240-1397

In Canada
P.O. Box 603
Fort Erie, Ontario
L2A 5X3

Take 4 books & a surprise gift FREE

SPECIAL LIMITED-TIME OFFER

Mail to   **Harlequin Reader Service**®

In the U.S.   In Canada
901 Fuhrmann Blvd.   P.O. Box 609
P.O. Box 1394   Fort Erie, Ontario
Buffalo, N.Y. 14240-1394   L2A 5X3

YES!   Please send me 4 free Harlequin Superromance®
novels and my free surprise gift. Then send me 4 brand-new novels
every month as they come off the presses. Bill me at the low price
of $2.50 each*—a 9% saving off the retail price. There is no
minimum number of books I must purchase. I can always return a
shipment and cancel at any time. Even if I never buy another
book from Harlequin, the 4 free novels and the surprise gift are
mine to keep forever.   134 BPS BP7S

*Plus 49¢ postage and handling per shipment in Canada.

Name _____ (PLEASE PRINT)

Address _____ Apt. No. _____

City _____ State/Prov. _____ Zip/Postal Code _____

This offer is limited to one order per household and not valid to present
subscribers. Price is subject to change.   DOSR-SUB-1A

PATRICIA MATTHEWS

America's First Lady of Romance upholds her long standing reputation as a bestselling romance novelist with ...

Caught in the steamy heat of America's New South, Rebecca Trenton finds herself torn between two brothers—she yearns for one but a dark secret binds her to the other.

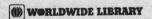